More Letters to Uncle Albert

More Letters to Uncle Albert

with replies from Russell Stannard

faber and faber
LONDON · BOSTON

First published in Great Britain in 1997
by Faber and Faber Limited
3 Queen Square London WC1N 3AU

Typeset by Faber and Faber Ltd
Printed and bound in Great Britain by
Mackays of Chatham PLC, Chatham Kent

A CIP record for this book
is available from the British Library

ISBN 0–571–19051–0

10 9 8 7 6 5 4 3 2 1

Contents

Acknowledgements

Thanks from Uncle Albert and myself to all of you who have come up with the questions, and supplied the extra pictures and drawings.

As for my wife, Maggi, I'm happy to say she still puts up with it all!

Foreword

The idea for this series arose out of the letters I receive from young readers of my Uncle Albert books. Many of them ask fascinating questions – some scientific, others not.

As with the earlier book, *Letters to Uncle Albert*, I attempt to answer these questions as honestly as I can, on behalf of Uncle Albert. If sometimes I get floored, please remember there are questions to which *no one* has the answer – and it always seems to be *children* who come up with them!

Gravity

I would like to know WHY is the world a sphere why cant it be a pyramid, a cylinder, a cuboid or a triangular prism.

yours sincerly

Natalie Moon

Everything pulls on everything else. If you have two objects placed in space, it doesn't matter what they are (two atoms, two elephants, you and me), each pulls on the other; they try to come together. The pulling force is called *gravity*. The more massive an object, the stronger its gravity force. And the closer the two objects, the stronger the force becomes.

The Earth originally formed out of a cloud of dust and gas. Each particle of the cloud pulled on every other particle. They got closer and closer together, and the gravity forces got stronger and stronger. The bits of dust and stuff pressed into each other and tried to pack as close together as they possibly could. And the way to pack things tightly, so that they are as close to each other as they can get, is to have them form a round ball. After all, if you think of what happens in a game of rugby, when all the players pile in on top of each other, all trying to get to the ball, they end up as a heap – a more-or-less round heap. That is why the Earth, and the planets, and the Sun and Moon all ended up round.

I wondered, Why don't things roll
up hill. They roll down so why
don't they roll up.

yours sincerely

Sophie Hibbs (Age 10)

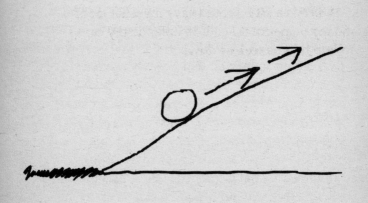

It's all due to this gravity force I was telling Natalie about. Things on a hill are like the bits of dust that originally came together to form the Earth. Just as all those bits tried to get as close together as they could, so the thing on the hill behaves the same way; it too is trying to get as close in as it can to all the rest. OK, the stuff that makes up the *top* of the hill is pulling it in the opposite direction: upwards. But all the rest of the Earth is pulling it down. So it is little wonder that it is the rest of the Earth that wins, and the thing rolls down rather than up.

Which is a pity. I could save myself a lot of money on petrol if I could persuade my car to roll up hills as well as down.

I was sitting down watching a televison programme about the south pole and I wondered that if you were standing on the south pole why aren't you upsidedown?

yours sincerely

Angela Chahwan
age 9

All of us start out by thinking that the Earth is flat and horizontal, and that there is a special direction in space called 'down'. That is the direction everything gets pulled. Jump up in the air, and you get pulled *down* again on to the Earth's surface. As you sit reading this book, you are being pulled *down* into your chair.

But that isn't the best way to think about it. As we have seen, the Earth is not flat; it's a round ball. The Earth's gravity tries to pull you towards the centre of the ball. And not just you. It pulls on everyone and everything, wherever they are – at the North Pole, the South Pole, the Equator, or in between. They all get pulled towards the Earth's centre.

Everyone says they are being pulled *down*. By the word 'down' they mean the direction to the Earth's centre from wherever they happen to be on its surface. The trouble is, all their 'downs' are different! If you are at the North Pole, your 'down' is in the opposite direction to that of someone who is at the South Pole.

It's a good thing there isn't just the one 'down' direction. If there were, and it was *our* 'down', the people living on the opposite side to us would have to hang on for dear life. Not only that: think what would happen to all the air and the water of the seas and oceans as they got pulled round to the other side . . .

We have been reading your book
The Time And Space Of Uncle Albert,
and we all enjoy it. My favourite part
is when Gedanken goes on a tour of the
planets for her birthday.

We would like to find out how the
planets and sun stay in the sky, and why
they don't fall.

Please could you come to our school,
if it's not too much trouble. We would
like to talk to you very much.

We understand if you are too busy.

yours sincerely
Leonie Lambert.

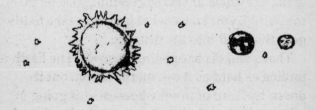

I have said how everything pulls on everything else with its force of gravity. And this force stretches right across space. It gets weaker the further away things are, but it is always there; it never fades away to nothing. That means the Earth and the Sun are pulling on each other – and the Moon – and the planets. They are all pulling on each other. So, you're quite right; you would expect them all to fall in on top of each other as one big heap. But for some reason they don't. Why?

The answer is that they are all going round each other. The Earth and the planets go round the Sun; the Moon goes round the Earth. How does that help? Well, suppose you tie your teddy bear on to the end of a piece of string, and then whirl him around your head. You are pulling on the teddy bear, but he doesn't get any closer to you. All your effort is needed just to keep him going in a circle. If you stop pulling (i.e. let go of the string), you know what happens – the teddy goes flying off into the distance.

That's what is happening in space. The Earth is pulling as hard as it can on the Moon, but it doesn't fall out of the sky because it is going in orbit around us. In the same way the Earth and the other planets don't fall into the Sun and get burned up in its fires because we are going in orbit around the Sun. We are all running around in circles – and it's lucky for us that we are.

How do you float in Space if there is only gravity on the moon and on the planets?

yours Sincerely

Philip Browning

The way astronauts float around in space is very confusing. When we here on Earth jump up into the air, we don't float; we get pulled down to the ground again by gravity. So, does that mean there is no gravity where the astronauts are?

No. As I was telling Leonie just now, Earth's gravity stretches right out into space. The astronauts are being pulled towards the centre of the Earth just like we are. So, why don't they fall?

The answer is that, with its rocket engines switched off, the astronauts' space craft behaves like the Moon; it just coasts along in orbit round the Earth. The Earth's gravity is still pulling on it, but the 'pull' is all used up in keeping the space craft going roughly in a circle; there is none left over to bring it down on to the Earth's surface. The space craft has, in fact, become an extra 'mini-moon' of the Earth.

The same is true of the astronauts. They are themselves coasting along, cancelling out the gravity pull on themselves by going in orbit around the Earth. But their orbit is the same as that of the space craft. So they coast along together. That's why, when we see them inside the space craft, or going for a space walk alongside the craft, they appear to be floating. It's a bit like two cars travelling along the motorway side by side at the same speed. To the passengers, as they look across at each other, they don't seem to be moving, but in fact they are both speeding along.

my question is;

why does gravity exist?"

from

(Eleanor) (age7)

I haven't a clue! Usually I don't like owning up to not knowing the answer. But this question is different. *No one* knows the answer – and that is how it is likely to be for all time.

The point is that scientists have the job of understanding and describing the world we live in. But that doesn't mean we can explain why the world is like it is, instead of like some other kind of world. So, I can tell you how strong gravity is, and how it changes with distance, but I cannot say why we have gravity in the first place. I guess that makes the score:

Eleanor 10 – Uncle Albert 0

Space Travel

NCC 1701-C

EX 1039-D

please can you tell me why do astro
nauts wear Space suits?
Mako age 8

Like everyone else, astronauts need to breathe.
Air contains a gas called 'oxygen'. We have to
keep on breathing in oxygen to stay alive. The
trouble is that there is no air in outer space.

Astronauts have to take their own supply with
them. The cabin of their craft is provided with
oxygen, so they can breathe normally. But if they
go outside the craft, to take a space walk, then
they have to put on specially sealed space suits
and helmets. Containers are strapped to their
backs, and these feed the precious oxygen into
their space helmets.

Could you please tell me
Why there is no air in Space?
Thank you
from
William Goock

It's due to gravity – again. The Earth, the Sun, and the planets all pull on the air and the other gases in space, just as they pull on everything else. So that's why you find the air hugging the Earth's surface, and not spread out evenly through space.

Because of this, you might expect all the air to end up flat on the ground – in the same way as raindrops get pulled down by gravity and end up as puddles. (If that were so, we would have to spend our lives crawling around on hands and knees with our noses on the ground sniffing up the air!) It's not like that because air is a *gas*. And one of the things about gases is that their smallest bits – called 'molecules' – are always rushing about like mad; they can't sit still for a minute (like some people I know). If there were no gravity to hold on to them, they would fly off into space like dogs let off the leash. That's why the air doesn't simply lie around on the surface of the Earth, but spreads upwards a little. The molecules are always trying to escape off into space, but they keep getting pulled back before they have gone far.

The air is thicker near the ground, and then thins out higher up. As you probably know, when mountaineers climb really high mountains they often take their own supply of oxygen with them and wear oxygen masks. If they didn't, they would be panting all the time and have to keep stopping to catch their breath. Modern jet planes have the same problem. They fly so high that air has to be pumped into the cabin so passengers and crew have enough to breathe.

Still, we mustn't complain. If the Earth had been smaller, its gravity might not have been strong enough to hang on to an atmosphere at all; all that jiggling and the air would have escaped. That's why the Moon and the small planet Mercury don't have an atmosphere – one of the reasons why they don't have any life on them.

My Birthday is the 8th of April. Im 5

HOW many aliens are in oater space

Love from Katie

This is a question I am always being asked. I'm afraid I don't know the answer. Nobody knows whether there are space aliens or whether we humans are the only form of intelligent life in the Universe.

Searches are being made. Scientists are listening for radio signals which might have been broadcast to us by aliens from another planet in space. But nothing has been found yet.

What are the chances of there being life out

there? I think they're pretty good. There does not seem to be any on the other eight planets going around the Sun. But there are lots of other suns. Each star in the sky is a sun (they look tiny simply because they are a long way off). And there are billions and billions of them.

We expect many of them to have planets going round them. In fact, the first planets belonging to a different sun have now been discovered! Of course, like most of the planets belonging to our Sun, they will either be close in to their star and too hot for life to develop (like our planet Mercury), or their orbit will take them too far away from their star and they will be too cold (like our planet Pluto), or they might be too small to hang on to an atmosphere. For any of these reasons, most planets will have no life on them.

But it is also expected that, by chance, there will be planets at just the right distance to have a nice warm temperature, and enough gravity to be able to hold on to an atmosphere. They might also have water. Given such a planet, there is at least a chance of life starting up. After all, we know that in the clouds of dust out of which stars form there is to be found the very kinds of material that go to make up our own bodies.

The first forms of life would be very simple to begin with – tiny, tiny things like bacteria. But with time these could get bigger and more interesting. Who knows, in the end they might finish up like us. They wouldn't *look* like us humans – that would be *very* unlikely – but they could be as intelligent as us. They could broadcast to us. They might even visit us! But before we get excited about that, we must remember that any space aliens would live a very, very, very, very long way from us. It would be extremely difficult for them to travel so far. It's not just a matter of saving up for the fare, the journey would take so long, they would be dead before they got here – which makes it all a bit pointless, don't you think?

'But,' you might be saying, 'what of UFOs and those funny circular shaped patterns in corn fields? Aren't they due to aliens coming from space?'

Well, all I can say is that you'll have to make up your own mind on that score. For myself, I think the corn circles were someone's idea of a joke. As for the UFOs, some of them are known to be hoaxes, some are known to have been harmless things like weather balloons floating in the sky. As for the rest . . .

Space

space →●

More
space
←

What is there when you go
through the clouds and you
go into space and then
you go out of space?
What comes up next?

Thankyou for helping me,
from

JOSef
(age 5)

What we *think* happens is this: You go up through the clouds. Then you go up through the rest of the air – higher than any aeroplane. Then you are out in space among the Sun, the planets and the space craft. Then you leave them behind, and start going past the stars (which, like the Sun, are great balls of fire). Then you go past more stars – and more stars – and more stars – and more stars – and more stars – and more stars – and more stars – and more stars – and more stars – and more stars – and more stars – and more stars – and more stars – and more stars – and more stars . . .
. . . . and so on, until you have filled up all the paper in the world writing 'and more stars'. Even then you have only just begun your journey.

In fact, you never come to the edge of space. Why? Because if you ever came to the end of space, what would there be after that? Nothing – obviously. But nothing is what space looks like! So it would be *more* space, and you would *not* have come to the end of it. That's why we think space goes on for ever.

However, we *might* be wrong! It might be that if we were to go on such a journey, after a certain time we would find ourselves back where we started here on Earth! How can that possibly happen?

Well, suppose instead of a space journey you went on a trip round the Earth. Imagine you are flying due East and you kept going and going in that same direction – always flying due East. What would happen? Would you get further and further from your starting point?

At first, yes. But after a while, when you are on the other side of the Earth, you would not. While still flying due East, you would eventually find yourself back where you started. It's all because the Earth is not flat (as it looks), but is really a great big round ball. Without knowing it, you were flying around a large circle, even though the navigator's compass kept pointing in the 'same' direction.

Now, we don't know, but it might be like that with space travel. Space might be curved in some very peculiar way so that, although we think we are always travelling in the same direction (a straight line out into space), we actually end up back where we started. That might be another way of never coming to an edge of space.

One piece of advice: if you ever decide to become an astronaut, think twice before agreeing to go on a journey to find out which of these answers is the right one. It could be a pretty long and boring trip.

What is space made out of?

Your sincerely
farah Morris.

Some people think 'Space is simply *nothing* – and
that's all there is to it.' But actually your question
is a very good one. The answer is *not* obvious.

To see why, let me ask you a question about air.
How do you know that, at this very moment, you
are surrounded by air? 'Easy,' you might say. You
show me by blowing out your cheeks. The cheeks
stay like that because of the squashed up air in
your mouth. Or you might wave a sheet of paper
about, setting up a wind. But note what you are
doing in both cases; you are *disturbing* the air. The
squashed air in your mouth is denser than that
outside. As for the sheet of paper, when it is
waved, there is more air piled up in front of it
than behind.

But suppose you sat perfectly still, and didn't
breathe. With the air undisturbed – the same
everywhere, it would be much more difficult to
know it was there.

Now I want you to imagine a kind of 'air' that
is *exactly* the same everywhere. And I mean

EVERYWHERE – it fills the whole of space. (By the way, START BREATHING AGAIN!) It's a kind of 'air' that, as you move, slips through you without you noticing it; a kind of 'air' where there is no pile up of it in front of you, or hole in it left behind; a kind of 'air' where there is always exactly the same amount of it whether you are thinking of a region of space outside your body, inside it, or in the far depths of space.

Such a completely undisturbed 'air' would be impossible to detect; it would be invisible. Why invisible? Well, think for a moment about this book in front of you. How is it you are able to see it? Because you can look at it from the outside. You can say 'It's here right in front of me on my lap.' But with the kind of 'air' we are talking about, it's not like that; it is everywhere; it has no edge; you can't see it from the outside because you can never get outside it. That's why it is invisible.

Now the amazing thing is that this is how we scientists sometimes think of space – so-called 'empty space'. We don't think of it as *nothing*; we think of it as a kind of 'air' that is the same everywhere. And because it is the same every-where, we cannot see it and it looks and behaves – like nothing!

'How stupid!' I hear you say. But hold on. I haven't finished yet. If this space-like 'air' *always* remained the same everywhere, it would be undetectable. If that were the case, I agree the idea *would* be stupid. But it isn't always the same everywhere. In very special experiments, scientists *are* able to disturb this space-like 'air'. We can actually knock holes in it! When we bash space really hard, we can knock a bit out of it; we see the particle we've knocked out (which used to be part of the space-like 'air'), and we see the hole left behind (which also behaves like a particle – we call it an antiparticle).

Who could have thought that *nothing* could be so interesting!

Notice

DON'T STOP READING!

The answers to the next questions
will be easier

Time

How are you?

How invented time?

Thank-you for comeing to our school and talking to us.

from
Reena *(age 10)*

The Universe was created in a Big Bang. All the stuff that makes up the Universe started out squashed together at a point. It suddenly exploded and came pouring out. When today we look at stars that are a long, long way off, we see them rushing away from us. That's because everything is still flying apart after that big explosion.

We believe the Big Bang was when all the stuff of the Universe was first created. Not only that, but it also saw the creation of space. Even that's not the end of the story: the Big Bang also saw the creation of time. In other words, the Big Bang marked THE START OF TIME! There was no time before the Big Bang. You can't even use the word 'before' when you are thinking of the Big Bang. 'Before' means 'at an earlier time' – but there was no earlier time.

That is what today's scientists say. But they were not the first to come up with the amazing idea that there was no time before the world had been created. Someone got there before them; someone who lived 1500 years ago and didn't know anything about modern science and the Big Bang. His name was Saint Augustine. The way he argued was like this:

How do we know that there is such a thing as 'time'? It is because things *change*. One moment the runners are at the starting line on the race track; at another moment these same runners are halfway down the track. What is the difference between the two? Time. What we are talking about happened at two different times. That's what we say. We can then invent clocks and watches which change in a regular way so we can measure the changes in time; we can say the difference in time is five seconds, or six seconds, or whatever it might be. That way we all think we know what we are on about when we speak about 'time'.

But, said Augustine, suppose nothing changes. Suppose nothing had *ever* changed. In such a world, would we know what time was? His answer was No. The word 'time' would not mean anything. We would not even *know* that nothing was changing, because there would be nothing going on in our brains. (So, it's all right, you wouldn't be bored in such a world; you need time to be bored.)

So, a world where nothing changed would be a world where there was no time. And as for a world that had not even been created yet – so there weren't any things *at all*, let alone things that *changed* – obviously there could be no time. That was how Saint Augustine argued that there could have been no time until the world was created. Clever don't you think?

Saint Augustine is one of my all-time heroes. If he had lived today I reckon he would not only have been a great saint, he would have won a pile of science Nobel Prizes as well.

('And he calls *that* an easier answer than the last one?! Who's he kidding?)

Notice

IT REALLY DOES
GET EASIER NOW

If the earth rotation was stoped and reversed would we carry on as normal or would we go back in time?

Yours sinserely
Gemma (AGe 10).

No, we would not go back in time if the Earth's rotation reversed. In fact, I don't think it will ever be possible to go back in time (despite what we are told in science fiction stories and films). Playing around with these ideas can be lots of fun, but if you take them seriously you soon get into problems.

Suppose, for example, you went back in time and found yourself driving a stage coach. While worrying about how you are going to get back to the present, your mind wanders and you accidentally run over and kill your great grandmother. If that happened she would not have been able to give birth to your grandmother, who wouldn't have given birth to your mother, who wouldn't have had you. So, you couldn't have gone back in time in the first place, because you couldn't have existed in the first (or is it the last) place.

Mind you, if the Earth's rotation suddenly reversed, you would still not 'carry on as normal'. Just think: the distance round the Earth's Equator is about 40,000 kilometres. The Earth rotates once every 24 hours. So that means someone standing on the Equator is actually whizzing round through space at about 1700 kilometres per hour (though of course it doesn't seem like it because everything at the Equator is going at the same speed). Now, suppose the Earth suddenly stops. What's going to happen? All the loose things on the surface (people for instance) will carry on at 1700 kilometres per hour, whereas hills and mountains won't. So the people had better watch out! And then there is all that loose stuff called seas and oceans. All that water is suddenly going to come ashore at 1700 kilometres per hour.

I reckon it's a good thing that the Earth is likely to carry on the way it is for a long, long time!

Black Holes

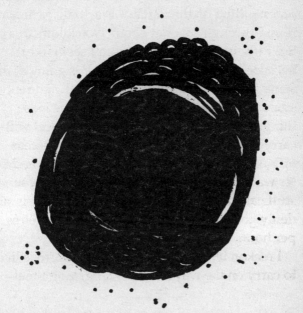

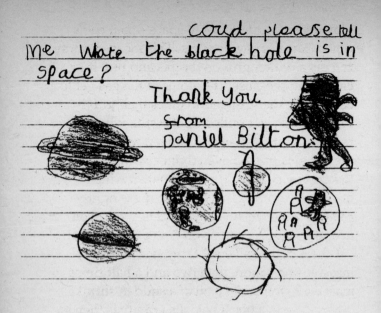

could please tell
me Whate the black hole is in
space?

Thank You

from
Daniel Bilton.

Black holes give me the shivers. They are really, really nasty.

What happens is this: stars are great balls of fiery gas, just like the Sun. As I have said before, they look tiny only because they are a long way off. If you ever got up close to one it would be so big and hot it would fry you to a cinder. Because it is so hot the gas jiggles about like crazy. It's only the strong gravity of all that gas that keeps it together in a round ball.

But, of course, a star can't burn for ever; like any other fire it begins to run out of fuel. The supply of heat is being cut off, but the gas is still glowing and losing heat to space – so it cools down. The jiggling gets less. This means gravity can get a tighter grip on the gas and pull it in closer. But the closer the atoms of the gas get to each other, the stronger becomes their gravity force, so they get pulled tighter still, which means gravity gets even stronger, which means the gas gets packed even tighter, which means the gravity gets even, even stronger, which means the atoms get even, even more tightly packed, which means gravity gets even, even, even stronger . . . and so on. You get the picture.

Where does it all end? If the star is a really massive one – more than two and a half times as massive as the Sun – it all of a sudden shrinks down to form a black hole. Its gravity is then so enormous that anything getting too close to it gets sucked in. And once you have been sucked into a black hole, that's IT – you've had it, you'll never be able to get out. Not that you'll have time to worry about that. You'll be dead – crushed out of existence within a fraction of a second. (I did warn you, black holes are nasty.)

In fact, gravity is so strong near a black hole even light can't escape its grip – that too gets sucked in. And if something gives out no light, it's black. That's why it is called a 'black hole'.

I have a question for you.

What is at the bottom of the black holes?

Yours sincerely

Lewis

Everything that falls into a black hole ends up at a point at its very centre. I don't know about you, but I find it absolutely amazing that a huge thing like a star (a million planets the size of the Earth would fit into the Sun) gets crushed down to something smaller than the point of the finest needle.

We are reading
" Black holes and Uncle
Albert " at the moment.
if you went in a black
hole where would you end
up?

I've been dying
to know this

Yours Sincerely
Oliver Ray.

You'd end up where all the stuff belonging to
the star went – at the same point at the centre of
the hole. (You say you're 'dying to know'. That's
certainly what will happen to you if you ever
decided to go into a black hole to check that I
was right. I suggest you just take my word for it!)

How come we know about black hols if you donut come out of them?

I want to be a scientist because it would be exiting.

from
James
Ockenden

That's a very good question. Not many people think about that. But you are quite right: no one can come back out of a black hole to tell us what it is like in there. Not only that, black holes don't give out any light of their own (like a star), and don't reflect any light that shines on them (like the Moon). So we can never hope even to *see* a black hole, let alone visit inside one. So, why are we scientists so cocky about them being there?

Let me begin by reminding you of the story of the Invisible Man. There was this man who made himself invisible; you couldn't see him at all; you looked straight through him. When he wanted to show people where he was, he would wear clothes and would wrap bandages round his head. That way, by watching what these clothes were doing, people could 'see' that he was there

40

in the room with them. Except, of course, they didn't actually see *him*; it was the clothes and bandages they saw. (If you get a chance of viewing *The Invisible Man* film on TV, don't miss it. It's in black and white, but very good – most black-and-white ones are.)

It's a bit like that with black holes. You can't see the hole itself, but you can see what it's doing to the things close by. For a start, many stars come in pairs. Instead of having planets going around the Sun, you get two suns (meaning stars) going round each other. Sometimes one of the stars, when it's old and burnt out, collapses down to a black hole. But this doesn't mean it's gone; the squashed-down star is still there, and it's still pulling on the other star with its gravity. So the bright star still keeps going round it in orbit as before. But now when we look, we don't see two stars going round each other; instead we see a star going round . . . well . . . what? Nothing? That can't be right; that's not what stars do. We know it must be going round something – even if we cannot see what it is, that is to say, even if it's *invisible*. Not only that, but if we measure how fast the bright star is travelling round its orbit, we can work out how hard gravity must be pulling on it to keep it in that orbit. And that means we can work out how massive the invisible star must be. It turns out to be *very* massive – as heavy as you would expect a star to be if it had collapsed down to a black hole.

(I hope you're getting convinced! If not, read on . . .)

I have said how anything coming too close to a black hole gets sucked into it. That goes for the atmosphere of the star orbiting the black hole. Its top layers sometimes get ripped off and sucked into the black hole itself – like bathwater going down the plug hole. And just as the bathwater gets faster and faster the closer it gets to the plug hole, so the clouds of gas captured from the star speed up on the last stages of their journey. They get so fast and hot we know that they must have been speeded up by an absolutely enormous gravity – the kind of gravity you could only get with a black hole.

As I said, we get to know that there are black holes the same way as we learn that there is an invisible man. (Except, of course, there *isn't* an invisible man – he was in a made-up story. We don't *think* black holes are made-up!)

I am glad you are going to be a scientist, James. It can be exciting, as you say. It is also a lot of hard work – but that's how it is with anything worth doing, don't you think?

How We Were Made

Hope you are well and your
brain is ticking over as well as
it usually does.

Why do we look like our
mums?

Yours Sincerely Jayne Braybrook

As you might already know, you were made out of a tiny bit of your dad, called a sperm, and a bit of your mum called an egg. When these two joined up inside your mum, you were on your way! You grew and grew. Each day you looked less and less like a blobby egg, and more and more like a proper baby. After nine months tucked out of sight in your mum, you were ready to make your appearance: Birthday Number Nought. That was the signal for everyone to start saying things like: 'Isn't she adorable; she has her mother's eyes, her grandmother's mouth – her father's bad temper, etc.'

And it's true. You *are* like them. It's only to be expected. After all, you were made from a piece of your mum and a piece of your dad; and they in their turn were made out of pieces taken from your grandparents.

In fact we now know a lot more than that. The important thing that decides what you look like is something in you called your DNA. The letters 'DNA' are the initials of a long name the biologists have given it. I can never remember these complicated names. But with this one it's all right because even the biologists just call it 'DNA'.

DNA is made up of a long chain of molecules. (A molecule is a collection of atoms stuck together.) Now the interesting thing about this chain is that it makes up a coded message. A secret code! Each of the molecules is something like a 'letter', and they are grouped together to form something that we might think of as 'words'. The order in which these words appear along the chain then tells the body what it should look like: 'tall', 'blue eyes', 'brown hair', 'genius brain', etc. One of the most exciting things happening today in science is the way biologists are unravelling the code – finding out what each bit of it means. It's a big job. A human's DNA has the same number of 'letters' in it as you will find in 3000 thick books.

Where did your DNA come from? It was made from copies taken from your parents' DNAs. That's why you end up looking like them with similar colour eyes, hair, etc. – you were built from the same set of plans. But your DNA is also different from everyone else's. It is a mixture of *two* people's DNA – your mum's and your dad's. That's why you are not an exact copy of either one of them. If your mum's DNA says 'green eyes' and your dad's says 'brown eyes', one of them is likely to win out – you will end up with either your mum's eyes or your dad's. But when it comes to the shape of your nose, or how tall you are, it might be the other parent's code that wins out. Not only that, but mistakes can happen as the original DNAs are copied, or your DNA might get changed as it meets up with chemicals in your body or is affected by radiation. Any of these will give rise to a brand new code. That's why there is only one you – why we are all different.

I have a big question for you. Do you now how people were made? If you now can you send a leter back saying. the question I asked.
thank you for all the things you have done for us.

your sincerely
peter Jackson.

Most scientists believe that you and I, and all the animals, were made through something called 'evolution'. Let me try and explain.

Let's begin by thinking of cheetahs. They can run very, very fast and that makes them good at chasing after zebras and antelopes, catching them and eating them. But not all cheetahs run at the same speed; some run faster than others. If there are not enough zebras to go round, which kind of cheetah will catch its dinner? The faster one. The slower cheetahs are the more likely to miss out and starve.

What makes some cheetahs faster than others? I was telling Jayne just now why children turn out to be like their parents. It's all down to their DNA. The same is true of the animals; they also have their own sort of DNA code – one that tells their bodies to grow into cheetahs rather than humans. Many things will make a cheetah strong or weak, fast or slow. One of these will be how much food it gets from its parents when it is small. Another is its DNA. Its DNA will play an important part in deciding whether it is likely to be a faster or slower runner than the average cheetah.

Those lucky enough to get the 'fast runner' code are more likely to find food. They will live to an age where they in their turn can have babies – babies that will inherit their parents' DNA, including the bit of code that says 'fast runner'. By accident, some will get a 'super runner' bit of DNA and outstrip everyone else. On the other hand, those cheetahs unlucky enough to have been born with the 'slow runner' code are in danger of starving to death. They are more likely to die before they have had a chance to have babies of their own. Because of this, the 'slow runner' code won't get passed on.

What this means is that there will be more members of the next generation with the 'fast runner' code than was the case for their parents' generation. We say that this code has been selected. The whole process is called *Evolution by Natural Selection*. No one is making the selection;

it just happens naturally. The 'slow runner' code just dies out naturally, leaving the other one.

In this way, we would expect the cheetah 'children' to be faster runners than their parents – on average. And, of course, when it is the turn of these children to grow up and have children of their own, the same will happen all over again: those that happen by chance to have a DNA that helps them to run faster than the new average speed will be the ones that will survive and pass on that DNA to the next generation. In this way we can understand how cheetahs have got faster and faster with each generation.

The same will be true of anything else that might help an animal to survive longer and have a better chance of passing on its own DNA code: sharper claws, stronger beak, tougher protective shell, etc. That's how we come to have our modern-day animals. All the wonderful creatures we see around us today have gradually evolved over millions and millions of years from much simpler creatures. Each of them has developed their own special ways of surviving.

But, you might be thinking, what is so special about us humans? After all, we are not good runners compared to cheetahs, we are poor swimmers compared to fish, we can't fly like birds, we don't have sharp teeth or claws, we don't have a tough shell to protect us.

The special thing about the DNA of humans is

that it gave us a big brain (for our body size) – a brain that can do very clever things. In the hard struggle to survive, our ancestors did not need sharp claws because they had the brains to design knives and axes; they did not need to run fast after deer because they could stand where they were and aim a rock or spear, or shoot a bow and arrow.

It is not that we humans have a bigger brain than any of the other animals; an elephant's brain is actually four times the size of ours. The point is that the bigger the animal, the bigger its brain needs to be just to keep the body ticking over properly. Because the elephant has such a large body, it needs a large brain just to keep going. The important thing is not how big the brain is, but how big it is *compared to the size of the animal's body*. It turns out we humans have a much bigger brain than you would expect for an animal our size. It's that extra brain size, left over after the body's needs have been looked after, that gives us the extra intelligence.

If apes develop in to humans what develop in to apes.

Yours sincerely

Alex Marks

(Age 10)

We think modern-day apes, like chimpanzees and gorillas, evolved from the same ape-like creatures that gave rise to us humans. You are asking what came before that. The answer is a small insect-eating animal. That in turn was developed from a reptile, and before that a fish, and before that little things like today's bacteria. We can't be absolutely sure, but it is very likely that it goes all the way back to slime and scum and chemicals in the sea! In other words, all living creatures (including plants and trees) have evolved from stuff that in the first place wasn't even alive.

The whole thing probably began when some atoms came together in the sea to make a molecule that was able to make copies of itself – rather like DNA today makes copies of itself. That was

51

the first important thing. Once that happened, the first of these molecules became two, these two each copied themselves to become four, the four became eight, and so on. The other important thing was that there were mistakes in the copying. That way you got different varieties of the original molecule. (Normally we think of mistakes as being bad – we lose marks for them in an exam. But it's a good thing these 'mistakes' happened, or we would never have been here.)

Some of these different versions had a better chance of surviving to make copies of themselves than others. These were the ones that survived and developed further while the others died out. The surviving ones became bacteria. At some stage molecules collected together to form cells, and the cells together made up the bodies of animals and plants big enough to be seen down a microscope. Over time, these became ever more complicated, until in the end we humans and the other modern-day animals arrived on the scene.

All this must have taken a very long time. But we know that there has been a very long time for this to happen in. The Earth formed 4600 million years ago. The first bacteria appeared 3000 million years ago. The first organism with more than one cell – so-called multi-celled organisms – appeared 1000 million years ago. The brains of our ancestors began to grow about 2 million years ago, and modern humans arrived about 100,000 years ago.

Was there really an Adam or Eve?

yours Sincerely

Louisa Silcox

11 years

It is certainly difficult to see how there could have been a real Adam and Eve if the theory of evolution by natural selection is true. Most biologists believe the theory because the evidence is so strong. We can examine the bones and skulls of dead creatures and follow out how the different kinds of animal have changed over time. Not only that but we can see how some kinds of animal are changing here and now; evolution isn't just something that happened long ago, it is happening right under our noses today.

So does this mean you believe in evolution if you are a biologist, but in Adam and Eve if you are religious?

That's how some people see it, but I think they're wrong. I am religious, and yet I believe in evolution – even though I'm not a biologist. Does that mean the story of Adam and Eve is rubbish? Has the Bible been caught out?

Certainly not. It all depends on what those opening chapters of the Bible were trying to say. If they were meant to be a scientific description of how humans were made, then it was wrong – according to the theory of evolution. But most experts on the Bible are agreed that the Bible was never meant to be read like that. In the days when the Bible was written, people just weren't interested in scientific questions. We might find that hard to understand today, but it was true of those times. (Come to think of it, most people today don't seem to be particularly interested in science!) So, how should we read those opening chapters?

The Adam and Eve story may not be science but it is saying important things about us. In the first place, we are made by God. (Today we would say that evolution was his way of doing it.) So, we owe our lives to him and should live them the way he wants us to live them. The story describes how Eve was made from a rib taken out of Adam's side. This is not describing a surgical operation; it's poetry. It is saying that man is not complete without woman, and woman is not complete without man. In other words, it is talking about *marriage*. It goes on to describe how Adam and Eve ate fruit from a tree that God had told them not to eat from. It was not that they were hungry; they had plenty to eat from the other trees. No, they were just being greedy, selfish, and disobedient. That again is telling us something that is true about *ourselves* – how we all have a nasty selfish streak in us. And so on. Those are the kinds of thing that the Bible is interested in.

Once you recognize that, it becomes very easy to accept the theory of evolution, AND what the Bible is saying about us. Both are true, each in their own special way.

My questions are, Why do people talk? When do they talk? Who envented talking? Who tells us to talk?

Yours
Sincerely
        Kathryn
            Ellison

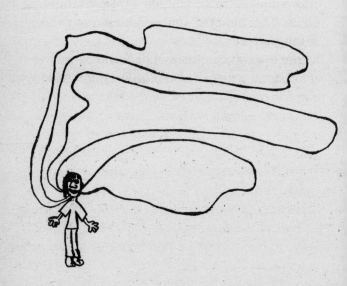

56

I told Alex (p. 52) how the brains of our ancestors started to grow about 2 million years ago. 250,000 years ago, the left side of our brain began to get especially big. That's the side of the brain that looks after talking, so we reckon that is when talking began.

Of course, lots of animals make noises. Wild chimpanzees make 30 to 40 different noises. Each has its own meaning, and says something important to the other chimps. I suppose you could call that a kind of 'talking'. With a lot of training, chimps can get across more complicated messages, and answer questions using sign language rather than voice. But it still doesn't add up to much compared with what we modern humans can do.

Like the chimps, we use about 30 different sounds (a bit like the sounds a young child makes when he or she starts to say the letters of the alphabet: aah, ber, ker, der, eee . . .). But, unlike the sounds chimps make, these don't themselves mean anything! The important thing is that we put these sounds together in different ways to make *words*. It's the words that can mean something. If I say 'table', then you have a pretty good idea what I'm talking about. But not all words have a simple meaning. If I just said to you the word 'but', or the word 'not', you would wonder what I was on about. But if I put them into a sentence, then they do make sense. In fact, it is the *sentences*, made up of strings of words, that really make the sense.

No one knows how our ancestors hit on this brilliant idea of replacing 'one sound = one meaning' with this way of stringing together meaningless sounds to make something that does have meaning. But no matter how it was done, it was probably the most important thing ever to happen to our ancestors. Talking makes all the difference between us humans and the other animals. It means we can learn from each other. When Mum says 'Don't touch that pan; it's hot!' you just take her word for it; that way you don't get burnt finding out. And not only can you learn from people you meet today, you can also learn from people you have never met; indeed, from people who are now dead! How? Through writing. Writing is a kind of 'talking' using books – like the one you are now reading.

Just think of all the things you know. Your mind is stuffed full of facts. But how many of those facts did you actually discover for yourself? Very, very few. Most of the information we have about the world is second-hand. It's what thousands and thousands of other people have discovered, and passed on to us – through talking. As I said, no one knows exactly how talking was invented, but it certainly was a brilliant idea!

Why do humans rule the world?

I hope that you can help me with the answer

Hilary

11

I get a bit worried, Hilary, when people describe us humans as 'ruling the world'. I think we have to be a bit careful when we say things like that. Certainly we are very powerful. We owe that to our brains, our ability to talk and learn from each other. That was the secret of our success as an evolved creature.

My worry is that being clever is not the same as being *sensible*. You might know someone at school, for example, who is top of the class, and comes first in all their exams, but is as thick as two planks when it comes to how they live their life. That's how it might be with us humans. We have this wonderful intelligence, yet look what we are doing to the planet. Look at the way we fight each other in wars. With all that cleverness we have invented nuclear bombs, and now we have built enough of them to destroy everyone in the world in a matter of minutes. It's clever, but it's not sensible. Perhaps we are too clever for our own good.

Dinosaurs were around for 200 million years. We modern humans arrived a mere 100,000 years ago. Will we still be around in 200 million years' time? I doubt it. If we're the 'rulers of the world', I reckon the dinosaurs were better at it than we are; at least they ruled longer than we are likely to.

When it comes to being a successful animal there are far more insects than there are humans. And when it comes to long-surviving animals, you can't do better than bacteria. They have been around for 3000 million years, and there are more different types of bacteria today than at any time in the past. Not only that, if there is to be a global nuclear war, it won't be the complicated animals like ourselves that will survive, it will be the tiny, simple, bacteria. Perhaps we should think of bacteria as being the true rulers of the world; they ruled in the beginning and they will carry on until there is no more life on Earth.

Not that I would want to swap places with a bacterium! No, it's good being a human. With our big brains we are able to live much more interesting lives than any of the other animals. But we do need to be careful.

How many atoms would make up my family of four?

Love from

Sarah.

Age 11

100,000 million million million million! (That's assuming your mum and dad are not too fat.) This is because atoms are so very, very tiny.

What does a big number like that mean? Imagine building a sandcastle. Your castle is so big, it covers not only all the beach but all of Britain – every square inch of it. And that's not all: the castle is 10,000 miles high! The number of grains of sand in your castle would be about the same as the number of atoms in your family.

Now you're asking: 'How does he know that?'

Well, I didn't build a sandcastle like that – obviously. But I did count grains of sand. I got a teaspoon of sand, poured it out on to the kitchen top, spread it out, took a knife and divided it into two piles. I then spread out one of the piles, and divided that in two. I then divided one of *those* piles in two, etc. That carried on until I ended up with a weeny, weeny pile. I then got out a magnifying glass and counted how many grains were in that smallest pile. I multiplied that by two, then that by two, then that by two . . . until I had done it the same number of times as I had divided the sand. That told me how many grains there were in a teaspoon of sand. Next I worked out how many teaspoons I would need to get the same number of grains as there are atoms in your family – and that told me how big the sandcastle would be.

After that, I got into trouble for having made a mess on the kitchen top!

Animals

could you tell me wiy cats
eat mice,
    Thank you from
    Jason Pickford

I have a cat named Curry. I love her dearly, especially when she rolls on her back and makes eyes
at me. But there are times when I can't help flying
into a great rage at her. That's when she goes out
into the garden and kills birds and mice. She
brings them into the house, and I see red. After
all, I know her tummy is full of Whiskas; she's
not hungry, so why kill innocent creatures?

When I calm down again, I realize I'm being
stupid. Curry can't help behaving like that. She
doesn't *mean* to be cruel.

The point is this: you remember how I was
telling Peter about the way we and the other animals evolved (p. 48). When it comes to surviving,
we are the lucky ones with the big brains, or fast-
running legs, sharp claws, tough shell, and so on.
These are all coded into our DNA. But DNA does
more than provide a plan for how the body
should be built. After all, it's no good a tiger having sharp claws if it doesn't know what to do

with them. An animal that has an in-born tendency to *use* them – an animal that kills on sight – is more likely to get food when it is in short supply. Another without that tendency – one that has to think it all out from scratch everytime – is likely to miss out on the meal.

So the DNA not only has codes in it for building the animal's body, it also has codes that tell the animal how to *behave*. And that is what is happening to Curry. On seeing a bird or a mouse she instinctively tries to kill it. She can't stop herself. It's her DNA that is telling her to do it. It was all part of her ancestors' survival kit. If her ancestors had not had this tendency built into them, they would not have survived, and Curry wouldn't be here today. The fact that those ancestors *did* have that code means that Curry has it as part of *her* code also – even though, since the invention of Whiskas and kind owners like me, there is no longer any *need* for it. These days it would be a better plan for cats to learn how to roll around and make eyes at humans.

Now, I don't want you to think that the kind of behaviour coded into the DNA is all about killing; it isn't. For instance, there is a code there that makes mothers feel especially protective to their children – even to the point where they will sometimes unthinkingly sacrifice themselves for their children. Then there is a code that makes the baby kangaroo, immediately it is born, head

65

up mother's fur to find the warm, soft pouch that is to be its first home. These are all ways of helping the young to survive.

Lastly, one of the really fascinating questions is whether the behaviour of us *humans* is also influenced in this way. After all, we too are evolved animals. Could it be that some of the reason why we keep going to war is that there is a fighting code in *our* DNA? Do we tend naturally to be selfish because our ancestors developed that kind of streak in them in their struggle to survive? They survived because they grabbed what was going, so today we tend to do the same. Could it be that the theory of evolution is coming up with the same view of us as being selfish as the Bible did long ago with its story of Adam and Eve?

Of course, there is one big difference between us and the other animals. Because of our intelligence we can look ahead and plan ahead. We can work out *different* ways for us to behave. We can *choose* to go against our natural instinct, if we think that would be best. So, much more than the other animals, we go through life planning and making our own decisions. It can be far more complicated living a human life than that of any other animal – but much more interesting.

why can't dogs marry cats.

from sinejib

age 9

The quick answer, I suppose, is that they don't fancy each other!

We say that they belong to different *species* (pronounced 'spee sees'). Animals that belong to the same species can generally mate and have children, but they can't with animals belonging to another species.

When we look back over evolution, what we find is that, over a long period of time, a particular species begins to split up. Some of its members develop one way, the others a different way. One sort might be good at surviving because they are gradually developing stronger and stronger legs and so can run away from enemies faster; the other might find it is developing a better grip and can climb trees, and get out of danger that way. After many generations, the two lots might be so different from each other that they no longer like the look of each other, and even if they did mate, they find it less and less likely that they will have children. Eventually they find they can only have children with animals of their own kind. At that point we say the original species has become two.

In fact, we think that all living creatures originally came from just one sort of ancestor. That's because all DNA codes are similar. Obviously there are differences in the DNAs of different species; if not, we would all look alike. But much of the code is exactly the same. That would be very unlikely to happen if we did not all share the same ancestor who originally had that particular coding. So, starting out from one species, this has branched out into different species, which themselves have branched into others. It's a bit like the way a tree starts out with just one trunk coming up out of the ground. That splits up into branches; the branches then split into thinner branches, which in their turn become lots of twigs. All the animals we see today are different twigs on the 'evolutionary tree'.

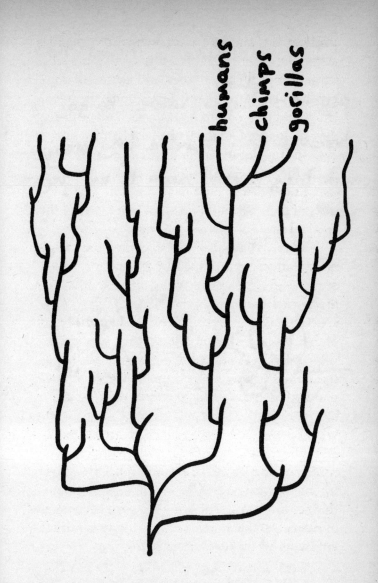

humans

chimps

gorillas

I would like to know how
pigeons and other birds know where to go
because they travel a long way
and they don't seem to be very
clever.

From

Vicky
Peplow

(age 10)

It really is amazing the way birds can migrate enormous distances to warmer countries down South in the winter, and then find their way back up North next spring. If it was up to us to find the way we would need to carry a pocket compass with us. That's how we would keep track of North, South, East, and West.

In fact, that is exactly how the birds do it! They don't actually *carry* a compass with them, of course. They don't need to; they've got one already in their brain! There is a part of their brain that is affected by the Earth's magnetism – just like the little magnet you find in a pocket compass. We know this because experiments have been done where a small magnetic instrument was strapped to the bird. The bird picked up the instrument's magnetism, as well as the Earth's, and got completely lost!

So, magnetism is one way they do it. But they also have another trick up their sleeve (not that they have sleeves, but you know what I mean). It's a trick of the light. There is something very special about the light coming from the sky. To us humans it looks pretty much the same whichever direction it comes from. But not to a bird.

Light is made up of waves. Usually when it comes towards you, the tiny waves wobble, or vibrate, up-and-down and from side-to-side. But with light from the sky it is different. The sunlight scatters off the air on its way to us, and this can reduce some of the wobbles; it might now be vibrating up-and-down only, or side-to-side only. We say the light has been *polarized*.

Normally, we humans can't tell the difference between ordinary light and light that has been polarized. We have to wear polaroid sun-glasses to do that. The polaroid lenses are arranged so that only the up-and-down vibrations get through. That means when you're looking at polarized light vibrating side-to-side only, it gets cut out; it can't get through the lens. (That's a good thing because sunlight reflecting off the surface of the road, say, is polarized side-to-side, so the glasses cut out that kind of glare.)

When you're wearing polaroids, if you look up at the sky, you will notice that the glasses cut out different amounts of the light, depending on which direction you are looking (even when it's cloudy). That shows the light is polarized.

The remarkable thing about birds is that they seem to be wearing polaroids all the time! There is something about the way their eyes are made that helps them to tell which way the light is vibrating – and that in turn gives them a clue as to which direction they are flying. So that's a second way birds can be sure of finding their way over long distances.

Of course, when they eventually get close to home, they no doubt look around and start to recognize the place anyway.

I Would like to ask you a question about Salmon. Why do Salmon know where to go after they have been swept down-stream?

from Thomas Butchers.

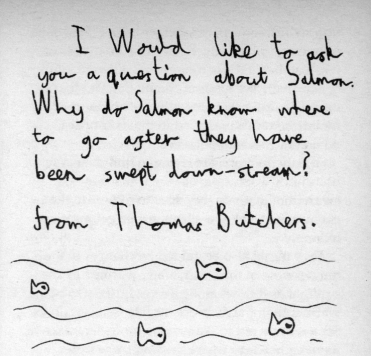

Having just read what I told Vicky (about how birds find their way around), you might think salmon also have magnets in their brains. That might well be true. Scientists are not all that sure at the moment.

But one thing we do know: salmon are very good at knowing what kind of water they're in. If you or I tasted some water taken from a river, lake, or sea, we could tell whether it was salty or

73

not, and if it was salty, whether it was 'very' salty, or only 'slightly' salty. But salmon do much better than that. They can recognize different kinds of salt and other kinds of chemicals. And that's useful, because there are different amounts of different chemicals dissolved in the river or sea wherever you happen to be.

So, when salmon are trying to find their way home they test (or 'smell') the water they're swimming in. Once they start to recognize the chemicals, they know they must be getting close to home.

They might also be guided by changes in the temperature of the water. Water warmed by the sunlight as it flows along a river is likely to be warmer than the deep oceans into which it flows. So, a salmon out to sea looking for the entrance to its river, heads to where the water is warmer.

Not only that, it can obviously tell which way the water is flowing. So, it might recognize the pattern of ocean currents. Once it finds the entrance to its river, it knows the river is likely to be flowing towards the sea. This means, to get up river, it needs to swim in the opposite direction to the current.

God

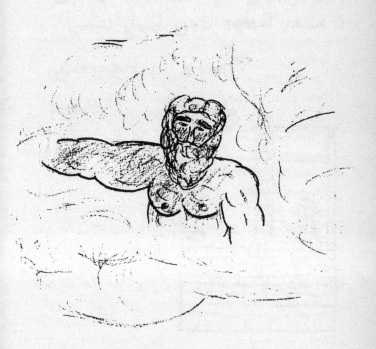

I was looking out the
Window When I thought What
does God look Like and
when is his birthday. Does he
look like a teacher or a
Child. Does any body now.

Yours sincerely

Christopher Hobson

(Age 10)

Nobody knows what God looks like because he probably doesn't look like *anything*. The trouble is that he is everywhere – like the 'space' I was telling Farah about (p. 27). You remember how I told her that she knew where something like a book was because she could see it from the out-side; the book was in one place, and she was in another. Light reflects off the surface of the book and travels across to her eyes. But with space, it was different. She couldn't see that because it was everywhere – outside her, inside her. It didn't have a surface for any light to shine off.

The same is true of God. We are told that he too is everywhere. He's not just in Heaven, but he's here on Earth too, and in outer space, and inside me, and inside you. It's a nice thought that he is always with each and every one of us wher-ever we happen to be. But it does make it diffi-cult to *see* him – which I think is a pity, but I suppose it doesn't really matter.

Long ago, when the early parts of the Bible were being written, it was reckoned that if you ever did get to see God face-to-face, the sight would be so extraordinary, so wonderful, so absolutely breath-taking that it would do just that – it would take your breath away; you would immediately drop down dead out of shock and sheer delight. It would be a great way to go! But I reckon it's probably best to keep things the way they are.

As for God's birthday, that is another way he is different from us. In order to have a birthday, you do, of course, have to get yourself born at some time. And God didn't. God's been around all the time. Not only does he not have a boundary in space beyond which he is not there, he also has no boundary in time before which he did not exist. So, no birthday. Not that we need to feel too sorry for him. When you're God and you own everything already, it would be tough thinking up something you wanted for your birthday.

how are you I heard you are starting a new Experament. I have a question for you is god Left handed or right

from

James

patterson

Age 11 years old

It's only natural to think of God as being like us human beings – only bigger and more powerful. Even the Bible sometimes describes him as someone who walks about and speaks like one of us. But we must never take this kind of talk too seriously. God doesn't have a body like ours. If he did, he wouldn't be able to be everywhere – he would only be where his body was.

So, I guess it's a case of 'Look! No hands!'

79

Two days ago, I was lying in my bed staring at the celling. I was wondering, how God was made, and who his mum and dad was?

Emily Hibbs
Age: 9

If you have read my replies to the last two letters, you probably know what's coming. You're thinking 'He didn't answer those questions about God properly; I bet he doesn't answer mine either.'

You're dead right! When it comes to questions about God, things get very difficult. It's not so much that we don't know the answers to them; it's not a case of 'Must try harder.' No, the problem is that we often don't even know the right kind of question to ask.

For example, take your question: 'How was God made?' It *seems* a very sensible question. After all, when we look around us and see houses, cars, plates, spoons, books, computers, etc., we know that they all had to be *made*; they didn't just happen; they had to be made out of something else. The same goes for people, animals, trees and plants – they too were all 'made' – they were born, or they came from seeds.

But God *wasn't* made. As I was telling Christopher, he was never born. There was never a time before he existed. Just because *we* needed a mum and dad, doesn't mean God did.

I sometimes think that when it comes to us trying to understand God, it's a bit like one of my goldfish trying to understand me. 'How come the water he's swimming in never needs to be changed?' 'How does he move without waggling his fins?' 'Why can't we see his fish food falling on him the way ours falls on us?' 'Which shop was he bought from?' If we find such questions about *us* funny, just think what a laugh God must be having when he listens in to our questions about *him*. No, when we're thinking about God, we must always be prepared to accept that the question we're asking might not be making much sense.

And this is not just true about God, it can also be the same when it comes to trying to understand the world. The sort of science I do is where we are trying to understand what everything is made of, and what space and time are all about. What we find is that when you ask the deepest questions about nature, you are likely to come up against a brick wall. You can't make any progress. Then all of a sudden, there is a breakthrough. Does that mean someone has at last found the answer to the question everyone has been asking? Probably not. More often the really great discovery comes through someone recognizing that it's the *question itself* that is wrong; it doesn't make sense. It *sounds* a sensible question; it is the same sort of question we have always been asking. But this time – at this very deep level of understanding – the question no longer makes sense. We have to try out some completely different way of thinking; we have to come up with a new question. And the first person to do that gets the Nobel Prize!

How do we know God
isn't a woman.

Thank you very much

yours faithfully
Sena

age = 12 yrs

That's a great question! Quite right; why should
we think of God as being more like a man than a
woman? I suppose the trouble is that in olden
days it was the men who got all the top jobs. So,
with God being THE TOP PERSON, it was natural to think that he must be some kind of super
man. But all that is changing. Women have
shown that in all ways (apart from heavy manual
work) they are just as good as men.

I think it can be very helpful to think of God as
being in some ways like a woman. For example,
we might think of her creating the world by giving birth to it.

What I want to
know is if there are any living
souls on other planets? Please
could you try and find the
answer. If so do they believe
in gods? Please could you try
and explain it the best you can.

FROM

TONY

FINN

(AGE)

(ELEVEN.)

84

As I explained to Katie (p. 17), I reckon there probably are forms of life on other planets that are just as intelligent and advanced as we humans here on Earth. Like us they will be able to talk to each other, and share their experience and knowledge. Once they have reached that stage, they will be able to think about more things than just how to find food, shelter, and a member of the opposite sex.

I would find it very surprising if they did not get around to asking questions like 'So, what's it all about? Where did we come from? What are we here for? What happens when we die – will that be *it*?' And that is when some of them will start wondering whether there is a God (or gods). They will start talking to God, and listening to him (or her).

If we ever do meet up with aliens, I reckon one of the most fascinating questions to ask them is what they think about God. In particular, people like myself who are Christians believe that God himself came to Earth as one of us – Jesus. So, did he come to *their* planet as one of them too? (And if he did, how did they treat him? We gave Jesus a *very* rough time.)

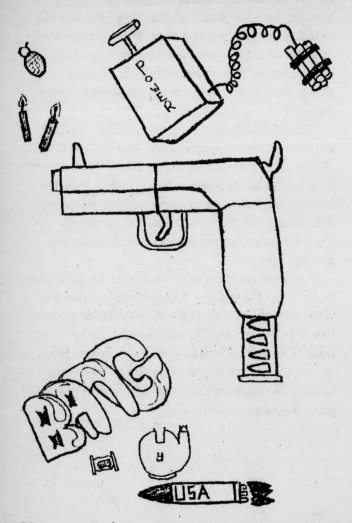

Love and Evil

Why are we kill each Other and no living happy an peacefully?

Best wishes
Ali Osman.

When I was about your age I was always asking that question. The war was on. I lived in London part of that time. Bombs were being dropped on us and neighbours were being killed. It all seemed so wicked and stupid.

And yet it keeps on happening. You mustn't just think it's the fault of us grown-ups, and everything will be different when you're grown-up and it's your turn to be in charge; your generation will be just the same. As I was telling Jason (p. 64) it is probably something written into our DNA.

Don't get me wrong. Humans are wonderful in all sorts of ways. But there is also something not very nice about us. The first step towards dealing with this nasty streak in us is to be honest with ourselves and admit that it is there. It is in *all* of us, not just in *them* – whoever 'them' might be.

Why were wer made When
god had made all other
things like plants, grass,
trees, animals, ants so on.

yours sincerely
Alexander Whitty

God is very loving. That is the most important
thing about him. He loves the world he has made
and everything in it – the trees and plants and all
the animals. But when you are full of love you
can't help sharing it with others. That's why he
made us: so that he could love us, and we could
love him in return. After all, I doubt whether even
the most intelligent of the animals can get as far
as thinking about God, let alone loving him.

I was looking in the library for a book for school when I saw a book about trees being cut down. Then I thought if god loves us . why did he let bad things happen to the world?

Love
Alicia Samuel

(Age 11.)

This is something we all wonder about from time to time. No one has a simple answer. All I can tell you is what I think.

The most important thing for God is love. But you can't be *forced* into loving someone against your will. So, to make it possible for us to love God, he had to let us be free to make up our own minds. But once he did that, he ran a risk: some people were likely to turn their back on him, ignore him, even hate him. God had to let them do this. Why? To give them the chance to choose to love him and live their lives the way he wants them to.

The trouble is God is not only a God of love, he is also a God of goodness. So, when someone turns their back on him, they turn their back on all he stands for – they turn their back on all that is good. And that's where the evil comes in. It's not God who does the wicked, selfish and nasty things; it's *people* who do them – people like you and me. It's not what God *wants* us to do. But he has to *let* us do it. If he didn't give us the freedom to act badly, we would simply be robots; we would not have the freedom to choose to be loving and good.

Not that I want you to get the idea that people divide up neatly into the 'good guys' who love God, and the 'bad guys' who don't. *All* of us – religious people as well as non-religious – turn away from God at some time or another in our lives; we *all* do shameful things.

In particular, as you rightly point out, Alicia, we do seem to be making a mess of the planet – cutting down more trees than we plant, using up the oil at a frightening rate (oil which can't be replaced), polluting our rivers and seas, spoiling the countryside, killing off wildlife. Why are we doing it? Greed. Pure selfish greed. We're all busy spending our money on new cars, new computers, new CDs, tarting up our homes, buying clothes, etc. We don't put anything like enough money aside for clearing up the messes we're making, replacing what we are using up, or exploring different ways of doing things. Greedy governments don't like doing anything about it because it would mean having to put up taxes, which in turn means greedy voters wouldn't vote for them at the next election. And so it goes on.

Mind you, things do seem to be changing for the better – slowly. People are talking about these matters much more than they used to. (Youngsters like you are writing letters to people like me about it!) I can now take my old newspapers to a collection place to be recycled. In the past no one wanted to know; it was easier and cheaper for them just to cut down more trees. I can now buy unleaded petrol. I have a catalytic converter on my car exhaust (I don't really know how it works, but I am told it cuts down the fumes). These changes all cost money, but I reckon it's worth it, don't you?

Death and Heaven

Pleasecanyoutellme
whydoesppeopledie
marvyn Iam7years ovd

Some people, of course, die as a result of accident
or disease. But I imagine what you are wondering about is why people die from natural causes.

I suppose the main reason is that they just wear
out. Take the heart, for example. It's a pump for
pushing the blood round the body. It pumps
about once a second. You can check that out by
feeling the pulse in your wrist. (I have such diffi-
culty finding my pulse, I sometimes panic, thinking I must have died already without knowing it.)
That means by the time you get to being 70 years
old, it must have pumped 2000 million times. No
wonder by then it's about to pack up. I reckon it
does wonderfully well to keep going like that for
all that time, without a break, and without a ser-
vice or overhaul. I only wish man-made machines

and electrical goods were as reliable as that.

When you think of how we humans got here (through evolution) I suppose it's a good thing we do die. If we didn't, then all those early ancestors of ours would still be around, taking up food and space, and not giving a chance to later generations to develop and become more interesting creatures – like ourselves. It's a strange thought that death is actually an important part of life. From the point of view of evolution, it is as necessary for all forms of life to die off, and get out of the way so as to make room for the younger generation, as it was for them to get born in the first place. In fact, it is now thought that just as there are codes in our DNA that govern how the different parts of the body should be built, there might also be codes that tell our body how it should die.

hope you can answer
my question.

why do people
die in graveyards.

by miranda
am 7

An animal that is thought to sense when it's
going to die is the elephant. When the end is
near, they are believed to go to a special place to
die – the elephants' graveyard. But humans are
different. Dead people end up in graveyards. But
it is not because people go there to die. They die
at home, or in hospital, or in old people's homes,
or in car accidents – in fact, they can die any-
where. It's only after they're dead, their body is
taken to the graveyard or cemetery.

With certain kinds of disease, the doctor knows
from experience that once patients reach a particular stage they never live much longer. In these
cases, it *is* possible to know when someone is

going to die. The big question is whether they should be told. If *you* were such a patient, would you prefer to be told, or not?

Even if you did not have a disease like that, would you, in any case, like to know exactly when you were going to die? I have often thought about that, and can never make up my mind. In some ways I think it is better not to know. But, of course, if you *did* know, you could be sure to get the best out of whatever time is left to you. Perhaps that is the best way to live anyway: you pretend that every day is to be your last, so that you live it to the full.

On second thoughts, if you did *that*, you would never bother to do tomorrow's homework, you would never revise for exams, you wouldn't bother to brush your teeth, you wouldn't save money for Christmas presents, etc., etc. No. Forget I said that.

Are there such things as Ghosts?
At first I never believed it but
I want to know for sure If
there are.

I can hardly wait for
you to come to our school
because I've never met a
professor before

Your Sincerly
Simon Sadlk
(Age 11)

When I was your age I had to walk down a narrow lane to get to school. At the end of the lane, just before it opened out on to the main road where the school was, there was an old building. It wasn't a house; it wasn't a shop; it didn't look like offices. In all the years I walked past it, I never saw anyone go in, or anyone come out. The windows always looked as though they needed a good clean. No one seemed to know what the building was for. We kids said it was haunted. It was exactly the sort of place that *ought* to have been haunted.

Whether I *really* believed it was haunted I can't remember now. I suspect not. Certainly I never *saw* a ghost. So, from my own experience I can't say whether there are ghosts or not. Perhaps people do sometimes come back from the dead. But if they do, I doubt that they are the spooky, sheet-flapping, trick-playing, carry-your-head-under-your-arm, type of ghost.

The most important thing of my
Life is when someone dies if they
are really close to you in your
family. my nan died and she came
back to me. When I lived in
no. 52 my nan came to me
when I was asleep. I woke up
in the night and she was at
the end of the bed. She was
trying to talk to me and I
was seeing her. but my mum
came in and my mum did not
see her.
Please can you tell me how it
happens. I have been frightened,
but now I am used to it

Please help me.
Especially from tracy.

I don't know what to say to you, Tracy.

Some people might think that you had not properly woken up when you saw your nan – it was a vivid kind of dream – the sort you sometimes get when you are half asleep/half awake. Dreams can appear to be very real.

But perhaps it wasn't a dream. When a very close relative or friend dies, there are times when they still seem to be around. Occasionally I find myself sort of talking to them in my thoughts. Is it just habit, or can they know what I am saying to them? They never talk back, and I never see them, but who knows, perhaps they still hear.

I have always believed that death is not the end of everything. Those who have died – like your nan – still live on in some kind of way none of us can understand yet. Perhaps your nan appearing to you like that shows they can still be close by. Whatever the true explanation, there is certainly no need to be frightened.

If we didn't die then people would be more happier Like I would be much more happier if my nanny was alive because shes never seen me and I never seen her.

My mum said my nanny would of spoiled me.

If god Loves us then why dose he Let us die.

Yours sincerely

Danielle Porter

You say we would all be happier if we did not die. I'm not so sure. It depends a bit, I suppose, on whether you just keep living on and on as an old

. . . then very old . . . then mega old person, stuck in a wheel chair, going more and more blind, deaf, and ga-ga. That doesn't sound much fun to me. And even if we were allowed to keep our young fit bodies, I'm still not sure it would be a good idea to stick around too long. Wouldn't we get bored doing the same thing over and over again? Only the other day I was in the local video rental shop and thought 'I've seen all the good ones already. I've lived too long!'

Then there are other problems. If nobody died, and new people kept being born, the population would keep going up. We would have to build more houses for them to live in, and more roads for all the extra cars. So, there wouldn't be as much countryside. But then where would we grow all the extra food needed? You only have to think about this for a short while to realize that things would get into a *terrible* mess, if we older people didn't pack it in at some stage.

Besides, does it matter if we die? Death doesn't have to be the end. I reckon once we are dead we shall discover that what we have been calling 'life' was just the soup course. The main dish (and the pudding) is still to come. Then we shall no longer be complaining to God about him letting us die; we shall be having a go at him for having left us down on Earth so long!

What i would like to know as how do people get resurrected? Because i'm very curious and how is it possible? Please try and find out so that i can read about it please.

From

Tony Finn

(Age) (Eleven)

Nobody really knows.

I can tell you what resurrection *isn't*. It is not a case of God gathering together the bits of our old body and making *that* come alive again. Which is just as well because it would be very difficult, even for God. Once the coffin has rotted away and the worms have got in and had a meal out of the corpse, it has now become part of *their* bodies. So, whose body is it now? As for getting cremated . . .

No, we are told in the Bible that when we are resurrected we get a completely new kind of body. We shall still be the same *person*, but we shall have a different way of appearing to God and to each other – a different way of being recognized.

It's a bit like an advertising slogan, or any other message. You first see it in the newspapers: 'The great taste of Pepsi', or whatever it might be. But then after several months running the newspaper campaign, the advertising agency decides to switch to some other medium. Next you see the slogan up in neon lights in the town square. Neon lights, of course, are nothing like newsprint. But it is exactly the same message. It has exactly the same effect on people – they rush off and drink lots of Pepsi. Some time later you go to the cinema and you are hit by the same slogan in the ads they show before the main film. Again it is a different medium. This time it is not even in writing; a woman in a bikini holds up the can and tells you face-to-face. But again it's the same message.

What I am saying is that whether the message is carried by newsprint, neon lights, or film doesn't matter in the slightest. It is the message itself that counts.

Now, I think resurrection is like that. You are a kind of 'message'. At the present time it is being carried in your physical body. But it doesn't have to be. It can be transferred unchanged to some other medium – some kind of 'heavenly body'. How God does this switch I haven't a clue – and nobody does. But then again, we have no idea how he created the physical world – and yet it's here.

I was sitting in my Nano garden looking at the sky, When it suddenly occurred to me, has anybody found heaven on a plane or on a rocket? So I ran in to ask my Nan, she said "that can't be answered" and I'm asking you, can YOU answer me?

Yours Sincerley
Marisma Sastre (age10)

When the first Russian astronaut went up, he radioed back to say he couldn't see Heaven up there. I suppose he thought he was being clever, or funny, or something. But actually he was being silly. Heaven is not up there at all – even though we sometimes talk as though it were.

In order for something to be real it doesn't have to be in space; it doesn't have to take up room. Thoughts, for example: we talk of making 'big' decisions (like getting married) and 'small' decisions (like deciding which T-shirt to wear). But that's not to say the big decision is, say, 5 kilometres wide, while the small one is smaller than a 5p coin. Decisions, like any other kind of thought, don't take up any space at all. They're simply not the kind of thing you find in space.

We often use words to mean more than one thing. We say someone has a 'hot' temper – but it is not a hotness that would show up on a thermometer. We say someone is 'sweet' natured, but we don't lick them like a lollipop. No, what we are doing is borrowing words that have one set of meanings when we are talking of physical things (like temperature, and taste), but mean something else when we talk about what people are like. The same goes for talk about people who have died. We use words such as 'gone up to Heaven', but that doesn't mean they have actually gone UP. It simply means they are now with God in a special way.

My dog TESS has JUst died
Last Wednesday, she died Of
old age and I would Like
to know Where and wat
Tess is doing in duggy heven?
Every time I am out in
the Playground I think a boue
Tess.

I am 6
Love Karriane

Tess

Some people say that animals don't go to Heaven – only humans do. It's not that these people don't like animals. It's just that Heaven is all about enjoying being with God. So, if an animal doesn't know anything about God, and found itself in Heaven, it wouldn't have a clue what was going on. It would just get bored. And as Heaven lasts for ever, that would be REALLY boring. So, if that is the case, it would be better for Tess if she has just 'gone to sleep'.

But who knows? Perhaps the more intelligent of the animals do, in their own kind of way, sense God being around. After all, they can't be all that different from us humans; we have all evolved from the same ancestors originally. So, if they do have some inkling about God, I see no reason why they shouldn't enjoy Heaven.

As for what Tess is doing there, I wouldn't know. I don't even know what it's going to be like for us humans. Some say we shall just be in a state of happiness. Not much (if anything at all) will happen. We'll just be happy to be with God. I'm not so sure about that. I like *doing* things. As soon as I have finished one job – like writing this book – I'm on to the next. My idea of Heaven is to arrive there and be handed a long list of urgent jobs God wants me to get on with! But I doubt that it will be like that. God probably has something even better in mind that I can't even begin to imagine.

why does the Water in the bath
go round and round When you pall
the the plug out? I What to Know
this because ellrey Wednesday and
Sunday I alwas puzzyl this and
my zamley do to.

yours Sincerely
Rebecca
Bullen

It is the same reason why an ice-skater spins
faster as she pulls her arms in closer to her body.
She starts by turning slowly with her arms
stretched out, and then speeds up. This is
because of her *angular momentum*. Angular

momentum depends on how fast she spins (the number of turns per minute), and how spread out her body is. If she squashes herself down, then she has to spin faster to keep the same angular momentum.

Now, what has this to do with your bath-water? Well, when you get out of the bath, you set the water swirling about. As far as the plug hole is concerned the water is slowly rotating round it, either clockwise or anti-clockwise. But at this stage the water is spread out over the whole bath. Eventually it all has to go out through the same narrow hole; it has to squash down, and that means . . . You've got it; the water has to spin faster to keep the same angular momentum.

But what if you got out of the water very slowly and very carefully? You would still find the water spins a little as it goes out. This is because, even without *you* swirling the water, it rotates very, very slowly because the Earth is spinning. The water spins one way in the Northern hemisphere, and in the opposite way in the South. Mind you, this is such a tiny effect, it can only be detected in a proper scientific experiment, where the water has been left to settle for *days* before the plug is pulled.

On holiday when I was practising my surfing in the sea, I kept on falling off my board into the sea. That made me wonder why the sea is wet?

yours sincerely,
Miranda Marsh
Age 9

Water is made up of molecules. Each water molecule is made up of atoms tightly bound to each other (2 atoms of hydrogen and 1 of oxygen, if you're interested). You can't see the individual molecules because, as I told Sarah (p. 61), atoms are incredibly small.

Not only do the atoms in the molecule hold on tightly to each other, but when you get a lot of molecules together, as you do in a droplet of water, each molecule pulls on its neighbours. You can see that from the way the droplet is round. (Remember how the planets ended up round due to all their bits of matter pulling on each other by gravity. With water it's not gravity that is doing the main pulling, but the end result is the same: the droplet ends up round.)

The molecules of water not only pull on each other, they can also pull on molecules belonging to any surface they come into contact with – whether that is rain water on a window pane, or sea water in contact with you when you fall off the surf board. When we say 'water is wet', we simply mean that water molecules pull hard on molecules belonging to surfaces like glass or skin. They stick to surfaces. With other kinds of liquid it is not like that. Molecules of mercury – the silvery stuff you get in thermometers – pull much harder on each other than they do on molecules belonging to the walls of the glass tube. That's why they don't wet the inside of the tube.

Don't worry about falling off the board. I think anyone who manages to spend any time at all on one of those things is quite brilliant! Besides, you always get dry again. That's because water molecules jiggle about. Eventually they escape the pull of their neighbours, and drift off into space. That's when we say the water has 'evaporated'.

I have a question for you and I hope you can answer it, why is the snow white? and why did we start macking snow men? and why is it so cold? Why is snow so soft like cotton wool.?

yours sincerely
Aimee

As I was just telling Miranda, water molecules jiggle about. They pull on each other, but also, because they can't sit still, they don't stay in the same place but slide over, and under and around each other. That's why it is easy to stir a liquid. But as the liquid gets colder, the jiggling gets less. Suddenly, when the liquid freezes, each molecule stays where it is, clinging to the same neighbours.

It's a bit like musical chairs. While the music plays, everyone keeps walking. But once the music stops, everything changes: you grab the nearest chair, sit in it firmly, and hang on for dear life.

That's the kind of thing that happens when the temperature drops below the liquid's 'freezing point'. Suddenly the molecules lock on to each other and hold on grimly. That's when water becomes ice, or raindrops become snow.

With our own game of musical chairs, the rule is one person per chair. If you grab a chair, and someone arrives a fraction of a second later – too bad for them. But with the molecules' version of the game, sitting on laps is fine. That's part of the game. If we were to play their version, then someone would sit on your lap, then another would sit on *their* lap . . . and so on. You end up with a long line of people all sitting on each other's laps. And the same thing is happening on either side of you; you get several lines of people sitting on each other's laps. And each line is likely to be different depending on whether the individuals happened to sit down facing left, or right, or straight on.

That's how we get snow. The molecules latch on to each other in a regular way to form crystals. All the beautiful crystal shapes are slightly different from each other because of the particular way the molecules latched on to each other.

So that answers one of your questions: snow is cold, because if it weren't cold it wouldn't be snow – the molecules would be jiggling so much you'd have a liquid; you'd have water.

Why is snow white? As we've seen, snow is made up of tiny ice crystals. These are solid and have lots of tiny surfaces. They reflect sunlight, in the same way as sunlight reflects off a window pane. The whiteness can be quite dazzling on a bright sunny morning, just as light reflected from a window can dazzle you.

Why is it soft? The crystals of snow are made up of ice, and solid ice is hard. But the snow crystals are all spread out, with long thin spikes; there's plenty of space beween them. So, it is easy to scrunch them up together, packing the ice crystals together more tightly – which is what you do when you gather up some snow and squash it down to make a smaller, harder snowball.

As for who it was who made the first snowman, I guess it was the first child to wake up and find it had been snowing in the night.

I was flying off to Kos (a Greek island) and I looked outside and the blue sea was so dark! Then I thought, why is the sea blue? Because when you pick up a handful of water, it's clear!

Yours sincerely

Gemma Harvey xx

Age :- 9 yrs.

One of the delightful things I remember about a holiday I had in Greece was the way the sky was always blue. And that immediately gives part of the answer to your question. The surface of the sea reflects the light from the sky, and if that is blue, then the sea will appear blue. If it's cloudy and grey, like it so often is in our country, then the sea looks grey and not nearly so inviting.

But the sea can also have a greeny blue colour

of its own. It depends on what salts and other chemicals have dissolved in it, and whether there is green algae floating in it. Mind you, this colour is only noticeable if you are looking through a lot of the water – if the water is deep and clear. If you have only a handful of it, it will still be a very, very pale shade of greeny blue, but you won't notice it.

It is the same with glass. When you look through a window of clear glass, you could swear it didn't have any colour. But notice you are looking through only a shallow depth of the glass – the thickness of the pane. Sometimes, a window gets broken (and I am NOT suggesting you do this experiment!). It is then possible to pick up a large piece of the broken pane – very gingerly and carefully, of course – and look through it edgewise on (so you are now looking through a big depth of glass). You should now more easily see the true colour of the glass, which is normally green.

Sky, Clouds and Rainbows

I think life is worth living.
There are many beautiful
things in this world and
I've always wondred
about rainbows.

How do they make
rainbows? How do they
get the colors?

I would lik to hear
the answers when you
come to my school to
see me and my class.

yours sincerely
Alexandra
Cooper

As you get older you tend to take things for granted. But not rainbows. I still get excited when I see one.

To understand how they form I must begin by telling you about light – ordinary white light, like you get from the Sun. 'How boring,' I hear you say. 'I want to know about the *colours* of the rainbow, not about light that hasn't *any* colour.'

WARNING: Don't be fooled by your Mum's washing machine with its labels saying 'coloureds' and 'whites'. Fair enough, it's important not to mix up white clothes with coloured ones when washing them. (I once forgot this and for months had to wear vests and pants that had gone pink!) But the amazing thing is that white light is actually the most 'coloured' light of all. It's a mixture of all the colours of the rainbow. How come?

Light is made up of waves. It has a series of humps and dips, just like waves on the sea. The distance between the humps is called the *wavelength* of that light. It's the wavelength that decides the colour of the light. For example, red light has a wavelength about twice as long as blue light, and yellow light is somewhere in between. White light is different – it is a mixture

of waves, all with different wavelengths. We know that because we can separate them out. How do we do that?

First we note that light travels at a certain fixed speed through empty space. It doesn't matter what the wavelength is; the speed is always the same. But this is not true when light passes through glass or water – the longer the wavelength, the faster the speed. That's good because we can use this to separate out the different wavelengths (or colours). We can pass the white light into a wedge-shaped piece of glass, called a *prism*. This slews the light round to one side so it comes out in a different direction. How much does it slew round? That depends on how fast the light is moving through the glass. Fast red

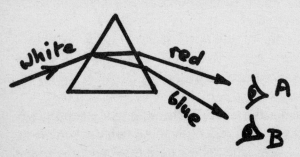

light tends to charge ahead so it changes direction only a little; slow blue light slews round much more. You can see this happening in my picture. If you imagine putting your eye at point A, you will see the red light; at point B, the blue. I leave you to guess where you would have to be to see the yellow.

Now, the same kind of thing happens with water droplets. In the next drawing, you see white light from the Sun being split up as it passes through the rain droplets and comes back

out again. I've shown you looking up at the sky. What do you see from that position? You are in line to receive the red light from the top droplet, and the blue from the bottom one. In other words, you see different colours depending on which direction you look. Different parts of the sky send you different colours – you are looking at a rainbow.

Quick Quiz

(1) Notice you need two things to be able to see a rainbow: the Sun must be shining, and there must be some rain somewhere. It's not often you get both of these at the same time. Why?

(2) I've talked only about the red and the blue light, but as you know, a rainbow has more colours than that. Can you name them?

Answers

(1) To see a rainbow, we need clouds to give the rain. But it's clouds that tend to block out the sunshine. So we have to hope for a gap in the rain clouds for the Sun to shine through.

If you have a hosepipe or garden sprinkler, of course, it's easy. You just choose a sunny day and make your own 'rain'.

(2) As for the colours of the rainbow, they are: Red, Orange, Yellow, Green, Blue, Indigo, and Violet. I've never really been sure about 'Indigo'. I reckon they just invented that one to give an initial letter 'I' so that the seven initials would make up a word that was easy to remember: ROYGBIV.

Except that 'roygbiv' is not a proper word. Mind you, I have always remembered it, so it seems to work.

Please can you answer those questions if you can't answer them thats ok. why is the sky Blue

Thank you

*Love
From
Tracey smith*

Age 9½

We have just seen one way of splitting white light up into its colours. Here is another.

When sunlight passes through air it gets scattered to some extent by the molecules that make up the air, as well as by molecules of water and by dust particles. The direction it bounces depends on the wavelength of the light: the smaller the wavelength, the bigger the bounce.

When you look at the sky right above you, what you see is sunlight that has scattered through a big angle. So, it is mostly the short wavelength light you see – and that, of course, means blue light. That's why the sky is blue.

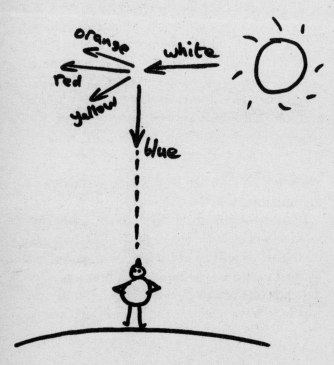

But, meanwhile, what has happened to the other colours: red, orange, yellow? This is where I can immediately go on and answer a question that you *didn't* ask, but one I'm sure you also want to know the answer to: 'why are sunsets red?'

Like the blue light, the red light is also scattered by the air molecules – but not so much; it's more likely to go straight on, as you see in my picture. That's why you don't see it when you look overhead.

But now suppose the Sun is about to set. It is low down on the horizon, and that means its light has to go through a lot of air close to the Earth's surface, with all its smog and dust particles. So there is a lot of scattering of the short wavelength blue and violet light (all right – and indigo). That means only the reds, oranges, and yellows have much chance of getting through to you. And that's why sunsets look red.

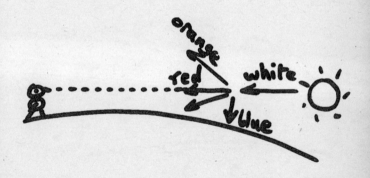

I was sitting looking at the sky. When it suddenly turned grey, and started to rain. I ran in the house and wondered why does the sky turn grey when it is going to rain? I hope you know why.

Yours sincerely

Hannah Ferguson xxx

Age 9 yrs

By an odd coincidence I happen to be answering your letter while flying in an aeroplane. I'm lucky today and have a window seat. Not only that, but it is not over the wing so I have a good view down below. That's the good news. The bad news is that it's cloudy. The pilot has just announced that we are flying over Greenland, so I imagine there are lots of spectacular snow-covered mountains down there. But all I can see below me is a blanket of fluffy cloud.

It is dazzling white. And that is the answer to your question. That blanket of cloud is reflecting most of the sunlight back up again. Only a little of it can be getting through to those mountains. If you were down there (Brrr!) and you looked up, the sky would appear grey. The thicker the cloud, the less light gets through, and the darker the sky would be.

But of course the thicker the cloud, the more likely it is to rain (or in Greenland, snow). So that's why it is a good idea to take your anorak when the clouds look dark.

What creates wind?

from Matthew Clark

I am 10

Wind is when the air around us pushes past us as it moves from one place to another. So the question is: why does air move around from one place on the surface of the Earth to another?

Near the Equator where the Sun beats down from directly overhead in the middle of the day, the ground gets very hot. This in turn heats up the air near the ground. (Just look at the TV weather forecast and see how hot it gets in countries closer to the Equator than ourselves.)

Now, the thing about hot air is that its molecules rush about like mad knocking other molecules out of the way. If the air is cold, then the molecules move about more gently; they can snuggle up closer to each other without getting knocked flying. This means a box full of air would have less molecules in it if the air is hot; more if the air is cold. And that means the box of hot air is lighter than the box of cold air. That's how hot air balloons work. The hot air inside the balloon is less dense than the cold air around it, so it rises.

That's what happens in sunny countries: the

hot air rises. But that's not to say it leaves a hole behind where it used to be. The surrounding cold air belonging to cooler countries like ours moves in from the side to take its place. That way we get winds at ground level. In time this air will get hot, it too will rise, and yet more cold air has to move in.

Once the hot air rises, it spreads out away from the Equator as very high winds. These, in turn cool, and come down in the colder parts of the Earth. So that way we get winds moving in a North–South direction between the hot equatorial areas and the colder areas on either side of the Equator.

But things are more complicated than that. The Earth itself is spinning towards the East. (That's why the Sun rises in the East.) This introduces a spinning movement in the winds too, and that's how we get the great swirling movements of air you see on the weather charts.

Not only that, you can get local temperature differences. For example, when you are on a hot beach, you often get a wind coming off the sea. That's because the cooler air above the cold sea comes ashore to take the place of the rising hot air above the beach.

Add all these effects together, and what do you get? A mess. (Who'd be a weather forecaster?!)

Please will you try to answer this question, what are clouds made out of? How do clouds stick together?

Thank you for trying to answer my questions.

Yours sincerely
Polly Glass

Let's start with puddles left after a rain shower. As the Sun comes out the water warms up. Its molecules jiggle about and some escape the pull of the others. They go drifting off to be among the molecules that make up the air. Normally we don't see them because a molecule is very, very tiny. If they bump into another molecule, they bounce off each other; they stay as a single molecule.

But we have just learned that hot air warmed

by the Sun tends to rise. So the water molecules are carried up by the hot air. As the air rises, it cools. Now the molecules jiggle about less. They don't bump into each other as hard, and they can now stick together. We have the beginnings of a water droplet. Eventually the droplet grows big enough to be seen. This goes on wherever the air is cold enough, so we have lots of water droplets. And that is what a cloud is: it's a collection of water droplets.

Actually getting a droplet to *start* growing is not quite as simple as I have said. Clouds form better if the air is dusty. At the very beginning the water molecules stick to the dust particles, and only after the droplet has grown a little, do they start sticking to each other.

As for what holds the clouds together, that isn't a problem. The shape of the cloud is just the shape of the region of the air cold enough to form droplets. So the cloud isn't really held together at all. There's no need for glue – just as you don't have to glue sunbathers together. You find sunbathers together on the beach because that is where it happens to be warm!

how do the Clouds stay up in the sky

Joseph ~~Coleman~~
Coleman

aged 8½ years

Clouds are made of droplets of water. Water is heavier than air. So, you're quite right: the clouds ought to drop out of the sky! And yet they don't.

I have a confession to make, Joseph. When I got your letter, I was shocked. I didn't know the answer. A *professor of physics* and I hadn't a clue why the clouds stayed up there! I felt very silly.

But it wasn't long before I began to feel a bit better. You see, I walked down the corridor at the university where I work, and I asked nearly all the other physicists your question. (I pretended I knew the answer, and was just testing them.) And do you know what? Not one of them had a clue either! Oh, they came up with all sorts of ideas as to what might be going on, but it turned out none of them was right. Not only did none of us have the answer, it had never occurred to any of us even to ask the question. That's often how it is in science. There can be some problem sitting right under everyone's nose (or in this case, sitting above their head), and no one even notices that it is a problem. Then along comes some genius - like my hero Einstein – who becomes the first person to ask 'Hey, what's going on here?' And then comes some big scientific discovery. Usually these really big discoveries are made by quite young scientists – those whose thinking is still lively and flexible, unlike we older scientists whose thinking tends to get stuck in a groove. That's why *you* came up with your question, and *we* didn't. (But don't get too excited; *someone* has already come up with your question, so you will have to think up another one in order to get your Nobel Prize.)

Now, just in case you're thinking I'm waffling on like this because I still don't know the answer, let me say I have now read a book on Cloud Physics and I now think I know what's happening.

Hot air rises carrying water molecules with it. The air cools and the droplets form to make a cloud (See my answer to the last letter). Because droplets are heavier than air, they start to fall through the air – which is what we expect to happen. But (and this is the important bit) the air they fall through is itself *still rising*. So in fact the

137

droplets tend to be carried *upwards* with the upflowing air (though they don't go up quite as fast as the air, because they are falling through the air).

Right. Now you're thinking 'OK. That explains why the cloud doesn't fall. But if the droplets are going up, why don't we see the cloud going *up*?'

The reason is that as fast as the droplets are swept upwards, more air and water molecules rise to fill the space they have left. It is now the turn of these water molecules to cool down and form water droplets in the same place as the first lot – before they themselves are swept upwards too. So, that way the bottom of the cloud stays where it is and seems not to be moving. But actually the cloud is continually *replacing itself*. As fast as old cloud moves upwards, new cloud takes its place.

It's a bit like what happens on the motorway. An AA man looks at the TV monitors, and reports severe congestion between Junctions six and eight. An hour later he reports that the situation has not changed. As far as he is concerned, the TV monitors are showing exactly the same sort of picture. But that doesn't, of course, mean that he is looking at the *same* set of cars. The traffic *is* slowly moving; the cars he saw earlier have been replaced by another lot, but the shape and density of the traffic looks much the same.

Going back to those clouds: the upwards

movement of the water droplets cannot go on for ever, obviously. What goes up, must come down – somewhere, some time. The upward moving cloud spreads out to the sides and eventually starts to fall. The air and its droplets are coming down. 'Ah! The cloud is at last about to fall out of the sky.' But no. As the air gets closer to the Earth, it warms up. And as it warms up . . . yes, you've guessed it. The water droplets evaporate; the molecules escape the pull of the others and they drift off once more as invisible single molecules. So the bottom layer of that part of the cloud also stays at the same height. Whereas to start with the base of the cloud was where new cloud was always being made before it rose upwards, in this other part of the cloud, the base is where old cloud is being destroyed as it falls.

The next time you see a speeded up film of clouds moving across the sky, watch out for this. If you are lucky with some of these films, you will be able to spot this sort of thing happening.

Finally, I should add that if the clouds are very thick, so the water molecules form really *big* drops, the rising air is *not* able to sweep them upwards. They are too heavy and they actually do fall. Also, even though these big drops are evaporating as they warm up on their way down, there is still some of the drop left when it reaches the Earth's surface. I don't have to tell you what we call *these* drops!

Lucky Dip

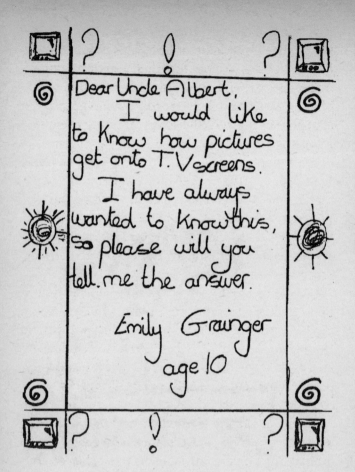

Dear Uncle Albert,

I would like to know how pictures get onto T.V screens.

I have always wanted to know this, so please will you tell me the answer.

Emily Grainger
age 10

If you look closely at your TV screen you will see the picture is made up of hundreds of horizontal lines. They are so close together, you don't normally notice them. They are made by a tiny spot of light passing back and forth. Wherever the spot shines, it leaves the screen glowing there for a short while afterwards; that's why we see lots of lines where the spot has just been, and not just the single spot. The spot starts at the top of the screen, and when it has finished doing all the lines and reached the end of the bottom line, it flicks back up to the top and starts all over again. As fast as the lines fade away, the spot returns to brighten them up again.

Now, if the spot were always the same brightness, we would simply get a plain white picture. But by changing the brightness of the spot, you can get it to 'paint' a picture. But how does the spot know how bright it ought to be at each point on the screen? That's where TV waves come in.

You have already learned (p. 123) that light is made up of waves. The distance between the humps (the wavelength) tells us what the colour of the light is. We said how the wavelength of red light is about twice that of blue. But suppose the wavelength were even longer than that of red light. What colour would we get? The answer is: none. The 'light' becomes invisible! But although our eyes are not sensitive enough to see it, it is still there. We call it *infra red* radiation, or 'heat' radiation. When we feel the heat coming from a fire, it is the infra red radiation that is warming our skin. If the wavelength is stretched out even further we get other forms of radiation: microwave radiation (as used in microwave ovens for cooking), and waves used for sending radio signals, mobile phone messages and TV pictures.

The TV broadcasting station codes a message on to the waves it sends out. Your TV aerial picks up the waves and feeds them into your set. There the electronics decodes the message. It is the message that controls the brightness of the spot as it passes across the screen. And that's how the pictures appear.

I don't know about you, but I find it quite a thought that the room I'm sitting in at this very moment (like yours) is full of invisible coded messages flying about: all the different TV channels, all the radio broadcasts, and all the mobile telephone messages. We would never know if it wasn't for our TV set, our Walkman, or our phone.

Why earn computers remember every Thing?

by Katherine Jackson

Keg 0

When it comes to remembering things, computers are like libraries. They store the information away in much the same way as books are stored on shelves. Each book is coded and the shelves labelled. A good librarian knows exactly where to find each book when it is needed. And that is how it is with a computer. All the information is stored away. But more than that, there is a system for knowing where each bit of information was put, and how to find it when it is needed again.

No one fully understands how our own memories work, and why they are sometimes so bad (mine is awful and gets worse the older I get).

One idea is that we have far, far more information stored away in our memory than we ever realize. It's all in there somewhere in our mental library; it is just that we don't have a very good system for finding it – we keep losing track of where we put it! That would explain those occasions when our memory is jogged by something we see or hear, and suddenly we remember some little thing that one would have thought had long ago been forgotten. But it hadn't been forgotten; it was there all the time.

Computers can get a bit scary. They have these amazing memories, and they can do sums and sort out information incredibly quickly. And, of course, that can be very useful for us. But take that away, and they are pretty dumb. After all, they're only doing what *we* tell them to do, so who really is the clever one? Mind you, whether it will always remain like that I don't know. No one can tell what the future holds. Perhaps in the end it will be the computers who will be telling *us* what to do. But we are still a long way from that. If the worst comes to the worst and they get really bossy, I suppose we could always pull their plugs out!

Why do 3-d things pop out at you when your wearing 3-d glasses, but don't pop out when your not wearing glasses? I've always wanted to know this since I was 5 years old. I want to be a scientist when I grow up so I can learn and explore different things.

Yours sincerely
Samantha. Lindsay.

As you look at this book you can tell it is 3-D; it looks solid. Now close one eye. The 3-D effect has gone. The book and everything else in the room looks flat. Next, open that eye and at the same time close the other. Keep repeating this: close left and open right; close right and open left . . . What do you see?

The book appears to jump about. That's because each eye is looking at it from a slightly different angle. And that's what your brain has to work on. It has to make sense of two slightly different, flat pictures. (Incidentally, you can open both eyes again!) In some absolutely marvellous and totally mysterious way the brain takes these pictures and produces a solid-looking 3-D book.

That's what happens normally. Now, let's *fool* the brain. Instead of getting the eyes to look at the solid book, we show one of your eyes a flat picture or photo of it, and at the same time we show your other eye a different photo taken from a slightly different angle. The messages going from the eyes to the brain are exactly the same as they were before. The brain can't tell the difference, so you end up seeing a solid-looking book again.

But we can't just hold up the two pictures in front of you; each eye would see *both* of them. That's where the 3-D glasses come in. One lens lets through only green light, the other only red light. So, if we hold up a picture where everything is simply different shades of green, it will be seen only by the eye wearing the first lens; the other eye will see nothing. In the same way a red coloured picture will be seen only by the second eye. In fact, we can print both the green and the red picture on the same sheet of paper and hold it up in front of both eyes. Without the glasses on, the doubled-up pictures look a mess. But with the glasses on, each eye sees only 'its' picture – and out pops the 3-D!

My name is Laura Sedgwick and I am ten years old. I like Science and I would like to know how we know what is inside the earth? Please can you help me.

From

Laura

Sedgwick

The obvious way is to dig holes and see what you come up with. But this only scratches the Earth's surface. The deepest mine is about 3 kilometres, and the deepest borehole about 15 kilometres – which isn't much compared to the 6370 kilometres it takes to get to the centre of the Earth.

A better way is to let the Earth bring up its own inside. This is what happens with a volcano. Lots of hot rock comes pouring out during an eruption. This tells us that the inside of the Earth is very hot. We can also examine the kind of rock brought up (once it has had a chance to cool!).

But there is another way. Suppose the postman delivers a present – a brown paper parcel. You are dying to open it and see what's inside, but you're not allowed; you have to wait until Christmas Day, or your birthday, or whatever. What do you do? You wait until no one's around, and give the box a good shake. With luck, it might rattle, and that could be a clue. For example, if it does rattle, it can't be boring socks and vests.

Scientists can do the same to find out what's inside the Earth. They give it a shake. Actually, they don't have to. From time to time, the Earth gives itself a shake: an earthquake. The Earth's crust (its outer layer) has cracks in it. When the two parts of the crust on either side of the crack rub past each other, that's when you get an earthquake. Earthquakes are very frightening and cause much damage. Many people are killed by them every year.

But there is a good side to them. The violent movements set up ripples, and these spread out through the Earth's interior. We call them 'earthquake waves'. They can be picked up at different points around the Earth's surface. The paths they take depend on what they are travelling through. They curve about and sometimes get reflected when one type of rock meets up with another.

When there is an earthquake somewhere, scientists all round the world record the waves it sends out. They then compare their results – what kinds of ripple they found, how strong they were, and how long they took to arrive at their particular point on the surface. Then comes the detective work. From all their results they work out what the inside of the Earth must be like. The picture they come up with is this:

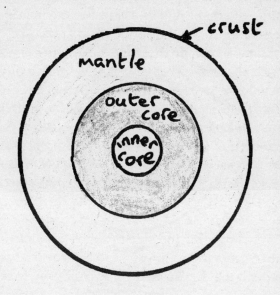

The inside of the Earth is a bit like an onion with several different layers. On the outside is the skin or solid *crust*. This is thick where there are continents (it can go 90 kilometres down under mountains), and can be as thin as 5 kilometres where the oceans are.

Under the crust is the *mantle*, which is made of the kind of stuff coming out of volcanoes. Then

2900 kilometres down (about halfway to the centre) comes a big change: we reach the *outer core*. This is liquid. We know this from what happens to a type of earthquake wave (called an S wave). S waves cannot pass through liquid.

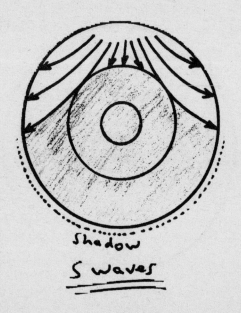

Shadow

S waves

This sort of wave never reaches the opposite side of the Earth to where the earthquake happened. This must be because it can't get through the core in the middle; the core casts a kind of 'shadow'. And the size of the shadow tells us how big the liquid core must be.

Then, at a depth of 5150 kilometres, we reach the surface of a solid *inner core*. We know of this because of what happens to the other main type of earthquake wave, the P waves. P waves can travel through both liquid and solid.

The inner core is slightly smaller than the size of the Moon. We think it is made of iron because

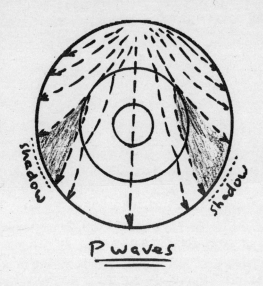

P waves

it has to be very heavy. We know how heavy the whole Earth is, and this tells us that the stuff at the centre must be about four times heavier than the lighter stuff we find in the crust. This points to it probably being mostly iron.

Finally, after going down for 6370 kilometres, we reach the centre of the inner core – the centre of the Earth.

My name is Varjini.
I am 11 years old girl. I
have mum, dad, and 2 sisters.
I like my school. Now I want
some qursten.
Who inventd numbers?.
Thank-you for read my latter.

Varjini

It all happened so long ago no one knows who was the first. In fact it probably wasn't one particular person at all. After all, even the more intelligent animals have some idea of how to count. For example, if a cat has a litter of kittens, and you remove some when she is not looking, she gets upset; she obviously knows that some are missing.

Almost certainly we get our numbers from the way people count on their fingers. That's the simplest way – the way young children are taught. Each finger is given a name: 'one', 'two', 'three' . . . and we can write that down using a squiggle, or symbol: '1', '2', '3' . . .

That's fine until you run out of fingers at 'ten'. What next? You start all over again with the first finger. But, of course, you have to remember that you have already been through all the fingers once. So, for the number 'twelve' we write it down as '12', where the '1' reminds us that we have already been round all ten fingers one time, and the '2' tells us that we ended up on the second finger. In the same way '23' means 2 lots of ten plus 3 more.

The next problem comes after 99 when we get ten lots of ten; we call this 'a hundred'. From then on we have to remember how many hundreds we've counted, as well as how many tens after the last hundred, so we get numbers like 237, meaning 2 hundreds plus 3 tens plus 7.

Now this is not the only way of counting. We could have decided to use the counting method that is still used by some South American tribes. They use the fingers of *one hand only*. They count: one, two, three, four, hand, hand plus one, hand plus two . . . We could write down this as: 1, 2, 3, 4, 10, 11 . . . Now the '1' in '10' doesn't mean ten, it means five. Similarly '11' doesn't mean our number eleven; it means five plus one which is our six. We say this way of numbering uses the *base* five, whereas our numbers use the base ten. You can actually use any base you like.

Please can you tell me why are you a scientist?
Thank you.
From
Catheryn Mears

When I was young, all I was interested in was cricket. I wanted to play for my favourite team, Surrey, and then for England. During the summer holidays I worked at the Oval Cricket Ground in London where Surrey played. I was even put in charge of running the main scoreboard when England played there in the Test matches.

Now, what has this to do with me becoming a scientist? Well, the point is that I used to go to the school that overlooks the Oval. (Sometimes, when they are televising a match there, the camera swings round – when the cricket is boring – and I can just catch a glimpse of my old school.) When you are in the building, you soon discover there aren't many windows high enough to see over the wall. You could see the cricket from the staff room (trust the teachers to make sure of that!). But the best view was from the *physics lab*. I quickly learned that in order to keep up to date with how the matches were going, I had to spend as much time as possible in that lab.

I never did get to play for Surrey, but I spent so long in that lab, I got hooked on to physics! So that was one reason why I became a scientist. (By the way, I recently visited the school and discovered that the physics lab has now been moved to a new building. The room overlooking the Oval is now the art room. Just think: if that had been the case all those years ago, I would today probably be an artist starving in an attic in Paris.)

A second reason why I became a scientist is that I had a super physics teacher. He had such a love of his subject that I must have caught some of it off him.

Finally, when I got to university and began to learn about the discoveries of the great Albert Einstein, they blew my mind! I thought I had never heard anything so marvellous. I wanted to tell everyone about it. I began telling adults, but it was a waste of time. They wouldn't listen, or if they did, they simply didn't believe me. It was all too amazing for them. (Adults get very set in their thinking; they can't take in anything too new.)

So instead I decided to tell children like you about Einstein's discoveries. That's how I came to write the *Uncle Albert* stories. And that's how you, and many other children, came to write letters to Uncle Albert (or to me) with your scientific questions – and other questions too. So, perhaps it was a good thing I didn't end up as a cricketer – or as a starving painter.

MAD Scientist

Fobbing Off

When I ask my perants
questions about flowers, leaves, trees
and wildlife I always seem to
get the same answer "it's just
natures way" so could you tell me
'what is natures way?'

from

Nicholas Gough

age 10

Goodness knows what they're on about. I reckon they don't know the answers and are just fobbing you off, hoping you'll stop pestering them.

Mind you, I can't altogether blame them. I've had four children of my own, so I know what it's like. Why? Why? Why? There never seems to be any end to the flow of questions coming from children. It's tough being a child – but it can also be tough being a parent. So don't be too hard on them.

In any case, help is on its way! Read the next page!

Just Before I Go . . .

Do you have the same problem with your parents
as Nicholas in that last letter? Are they too busy
to give you a proper answer to your questions?

If so, why not try out your BIG question on
Uncle Albert? See if you can stump *him*. It can be
about anything you like – but be sure it's a really
interesting question and one that has not already
appeared in either this or the earlier *Letters to
Uncle Albert* book. Send it to:

Uncle Albert's Post Bag
c/o Faber and Faber
3 Queen Square
London, WC1N 3AU

I can't promise to include yours in the next book in the series; someone else might have asked the same question, or there might not be room for it, (or I might not get enough new questions for there to be another book at all!). But it will help your chances if you write neatly. It might also help to include a nice black-and-white drawing.

Lots of love

Russell Stannard
(aged 64)

The Children

Jamie Beeson-Gould
Natalie Moon
Sophie Hibbs (10)
Angela Chahwan (9)
Leonie Lambert
Edward Davenport
Philip Browning
Eleanor Hughes (7)
Ahmed (10)
Christopher Moore
Marco (8)
William Goock
Katie (5)
Dennis (8)
Josef (5)
Farah Morris
Reena (10)
Gemma (10)
Daniel Bilton
Lewis
Oliver Ray
James Ockenden
Miranda Ike (9)

Jayne Braybrook
Peter Jackson
Alex Marks (10)
Louisa Silcox (11)
Jonathan Saunders (10)
Kathryn Ellison
Hilary (11)
Sarah (11)
Jason Pickford
Simerjit (9)
Vicky Peplow (10)
Thomas Butchers
Rachel Smith
Elaine Amielle (10)
Christopher Hobson (10)
James Patterson (11)
Sarah Webb
Emily Hibbs (9)
Sena (12)
Tony Finn (11)
Karima (10)
Ali Osman
Alexander Whitty

Alicia Samuel (11)
Luke Petty
Marvyn (7)
Miranda (7)
Simon Sadek (11)
Tracy
Danielle Porter
Gulsen (8)
Mariana Sastre (10)
Karriane (6)
Amy Rixon (10)
Ruby
Anna Rogers (10)
Rebecca Bullen
Miranda Marsh (9)
Aimee
Gemma Harvey (9)
Elizabeth Balsillie (10)

Alexandra Cooper
Tracey Smith (9½)
Hannah Ferguson (9)
Matthew Clark (10)
Polly Glass
Joseph Coleman (8½)
Bethany Hawkins (10)
Hemant Bedarkar (9)
Emily Grainger (10)
Katherine Jackson (10)
Samantha Lindsay
Laura Sedgwick
Varjini (11)
Catheryn Mears
Paul Reilly (10)
Nicholas Gough (10)
Kerry Stannard (10)